The City of Sacred Bones

Mara Beltane Mystery Series, Volume 2

Katie McVay

Published by Tamerlane Media, 2025.

THE CITY OF SACRED BONES

First edition. May 29, 2025.

Copyright © 2025 Katie McVay.

ISBN: 979-8989852468

Written by Katie McVay.

PART ONE
CHAPTER ONE

. . . .

PIAZZA SAN PIETRO
Saint Peter's Square
Rome

The cobblestones were still damp from early morning rain and tourists flooded the square. I navigated my way through the elliptical space, past the pink granite obelisk, and stared up in awe at the statues of the saints perched high atop the curved colonnade that surrounded me.

Suddenly a child darted across my path, rousting a pack of pigeons and sending them in a cacophony of wing flutters across the sky. I sidestepped the young boy, who frowned at his failure to catch one of the birds, and continued walking straight. The palace-like façade that was my final destination loomed in front of me, a behemoth of Renaissance mastery.

I had received an email from my Israeli friend Uri a few days before. He had heard about the success of my latest novel and wondered if I might be up for another adventure. Perhaps I needed material for my next book, he had asked. Maybe he could help me research that book too, he had suggested.

"If so," Uri wrote, "meet me in Rome."

He'd chosen Saint Peter's Basilica as a meeting place for a reason, but it hardly mattered why.

I would have followed Uri anywhere.

I trusted him enough to know that he wouldn't lead me on a wild goose chase, and, truth be told, I missed him.

So I hopped on a plane and flew to Rome.

During the flight I mentally prepared myself for the unknown, because Uri was always good for that: Ushering you headlong into a roller coaster journey of discovery. And when you start the journey, he warned me once, you may not turn back.

I was reminded of that while walking through the square. I finally spotted him standing near the steps leading up to the columned entrance of the basilica, an umbrella in his hand. As I approached, he smiled.

"Mara yakiri," Uri said. *My dear Mara.*

"Hi, Uri."

He looked good. A little grayer on top, but otherwise, Dr. Uri Nevon was still a handsome devil.

"It has been a long time," he said. "You look beautiful, as always."

I blushed and stared down at the dark cobblestones. Then, gaining the courage to face the man and the adventure he was inevitably about to lead me on, I said, "So why here? Why Rome?"

"There's someone I want you to meet," he said.

"Inside the basilica?" I asked.

"Perhaps." He flashed a devilish grin. "Perhaps not."

"I...I don't understand."

Uri took my hand and a pulse shot up through my arm. It had been so long, I'd almost forgotten how comforting—how natural—his touch felt.

"The person I want you to see may or may not be here," Uri said, looking me deep in the eyes. "But this is where your journey must begin."

CHAPTER TWO

It had been almost two years since I'd seen Dr. Uri Nevon. In that time, I'd taken a break from writing chick-lit novels, published the first book in a planned series of biblical thrillers, and celebrated as the first book shot up the *New York Times* bestseller list.

But that wasn't my original, intended path.

When last I saw Uri, I wasn't even going to write the novel he'd helped me research. I didn't think I could. Or should. I'd told Uri I wouldn't. Besides, the book wasn't the genre I usually wrote in. It wasn't what my readers were used to. And it was controversial. The novel had the potential to blow up in my face, ruin my career.

Instead, it did the opposite. It became a best-seller.

I celebrated by skipping town, hopping on a plane bound for Rome.

Not wanting to rest on my laurels, I wanted to dive straight into the next book in the series. I had a feeling Uri would be instrumental in that. Plus, I needed a little vacation. Going to Rome would accomplish both tasks.

My agent, Jenny, was less than thrilled by the decision.

"You're going *where*?" she had said.

"Rome," I repeated.

"What's in Rome?"

Uri's in Rome, I thought without speaking aloud.

"I need a break," I'd said. "And I need to research book two."

Jenny paused a moment before saying, "Maybe I should also ask, *who* is in Rome?"

"OK, fine. Uri's in Rome. And he says he has a great idea for my next book and the research material that'll help me write it."

Jenny sighed. "Uri..."

"I know, I know..." I trailed off, too.

"And this...*research material*...just happens to be in Rome?"

3

"That's what he told me."

"Mm hmm."

"Rome is loaded with biblical history. He knows the type of story I'm after. I trust him."

"Just don't be getting any romantic notions in your head."

"Not my intention, Jenny."

"Good, because he's a distraction you don't need right now. So if you insist on going to Rome—"

"I insist on going to Rome," I interjected.

"Then I recommend you get what you need, and get the hell out of Dodge."

"Wow."

"Just saying..."

"I trust Uri. He wouldn't let me go to Rome on a whim. He's got something. Something that'll make for another best-seller. I just know it."

"So what's the second book about?"

"I don't know yet. I have to go to Rome to find out."

CHAPTER THREE

I stood under the portico of Saint Peter's Basilica, looking into the deep brown eyes of Dr. Uri Nevon. Almost two years had passed without so much as an email between us, so I was unsure about a lot of things.

Was he still teaching at Hebrew University in Jerusalem? Was he still in communication with his ex-fiancé, Ziva, a fellow professor who'd broken their engagement upon learning of his near-obsession with the Talpiot tomb, only to marry the man who'd arrested Uri for breaking into said tomb? Did he continue his friendship with Lev, the young shop clerk and almost brother-in-law who'd helped him break into the Talpiot tomb?

Mostly, though, I wanted to know his reasons for wanting to meet me here, in Rome, at Saint Peter's Basilica. Perhaps most importantly, I wanted to know if he ever thought about me...

We had some catching up to do, and I was hoping a week-long visit would allow me to unwind, reacquaint with Uri, and get inspired for the next novel I needed to write.

At the moment though, I was distracted. As if Rome in the spring wasn't overwhelmingly distracting enough, Uri was holding my hand and looking at me in that curious way of his, with his eyebrows arched and his mouth set, as if waiting for me to say something. I'd seen him do this many times, as he stood before a roomful of eager students in a lecture hall, awaiting questions or answers or for lively debate. So while I sorely missed the affection of a handsome, successful, passionate man—perhaps *this* handsome, successful, passionate man—the city of Michelangelo surrounded me, and I couldn't help but think about the first time I found myself in Rome.

It was nearly ten years ago, and Thomas and I were on our honeymoon. We were blissfully happy and completely unaware that in a few short years our marriage would crumble and fall apart. During

5

our week in Rome, we'd gained more weight than we cared to remember eating pizza and pasta and creamy gelato; attempted to walk it off in more museums than our brains had power to remember; and marveled at the architecture and history of a city that, after the fall of its mighty empire, became the center of the Christian world.

I'd even thrown a coin over my left shoulder into the Trevi Fountain, the most cliché of touristy actions, thus supposedly guaranteeing my return to the City of Seven Hills. At the time I was certain that I'd return to this magnificently beautiful city. After all, how could anyone avoid the allure of a city that did nothing less than give birth to languages that are spoken by nearly eight hundred million people worldwide, inspired popular tales of love that changed the face of literature forever, and gave rise to the mightiest empire the world has ever known, and has yet to see the likes of since?

Yes, I was sure I would return to Rome, but naively I thought I'd be accompanied by my husband. But Thomas, never one to believe in superstitions, didn't throw a coin into the Trevi Fountain. His own volition would bring him back, he'd said, not an old wives' tale. Perhaps with his inaction and disbelief, our fate had been sealed. Because here I was, back in Rome after nearly a decade...alone.

But at the moment I had Uri for company. And I was wondering how Saint Peter's Basilica fit into the newest adventure he had planned for us.

"So...this is it," I said, spinning around to take in the sprawl and the splendor that is the piazza of Saint Peter's and the mother church of Roman Catholic Christendom.

"The most sacred of shrines," Uri said.

"You said our journey must begin here. Why?"

It was then that I noticed a man over Uri's left shoulder approaching us, calling Uri's name. Uri spun around, said a few words in Italian to the older gentleman, and shook his hand vigorously.

Uri ignored my question and stepped aside so the man could be properly introduced. "Miss Mara Beltane, may I present to you Dr. Giovanni Maderno, professor of architectural sciences at Sapienza University of Rome. He's the foremost expert on the history and architecture of Saint Peter's."

Dr. Maderno smiled and bowed slightly. He was the same height as Uri and slender, with curly black-and-gray hair slicked back from his forehead. He was, I guessed, about sixty years old.

"Miss Beltane, such a pleasure to meet you," he said in accented English, squeezing my hand firmly. "I've heard so much about your book from Uri. Congratulations."

"Thank you," I said, sliding my eyes briefly to Uri for any sign as to what was happening. I was expecting to have Uri to myself for the day, but obviously Uri had other plans. I should have expected as much, for Uri to have another surprise up his sleeve, but not so early into my visit. "I owe much of my success to Uri."

"Nonsense," Uri said, finally looking at me. "The full credit goes to you."

I searched his eyes for the answer that I was looking for, that Uri wanted to spend the day with me as well, but came up empty. He returned his gaze to Dr. Maderno, beaming at his friend and colleague with the pride of a young man looking up to his older brother.

"Mara," Uri said, still keeping his eyes on his colleague, "Not only is Giovanni the top expert on Saint Peter's, but he is also an ancestor of none other than Carlo Maderno!"

The professor straightened his back and raised his chin, as if to honor his long-lost relative. "Sì, è vero," he said.

"Who's Carlo Maderno?" I asked, looking between the two men for confirmation.

"He designed this beautiful façade," Uri said, motioning his hand down its immense columned length. "And he had the gumption to change Michelangelo's design."

"Ah, more like he was *pressured* to change Michelangelo's design," Dr. Maderno said. "But there is time enough for that, no?" Then, turning his attention back to Uri, the professor said, "My friend, you are getting ahead of me. You mustn't ruin the private tour I have planned for Mara."

"My apologies, Giovanni. You know how excitable I can be."

"Yes, and always so full of surprises," the professor said, turning to me. "Wouldn't you agree, Miss Beltane?"

"I'll say. Until two minutes ago I didn't know he spoke Italian," I said, and the two men laughed. Then, perhaps a bit too harshly I said, "And I hadn't the slightest clue that I'd be having a privately-guided tour today." At that the two men exchanged glances. I forced a laugh in attempt to cover my anger-laced words borne of disappointment. "So yes, I'd say our mutual acquaintance is a bit of a mystery." I looked at Uri, who only shrugged and smiled sheepishly.

Dr. Maderno chuckled. "I must admit I had a little bit more advance notice of your arrival than you did of your tour. But I would've agreed to meet you no matter how late the invitation." Then he turned to Uri. "Nulla per un vecchio amico, no? Anything for an old friend," he said, patting Uri on the back.

"Grazie," Uri said.

Dr. Maderno turned to me. "Are you ready for your tour, Miss Beltane?"

"Absolutely."

"Then I will be going," Uri said, looking at both of us in turn. "Giovanni, thank you again for being available last minute. Let us meet up again while I am in town." The two men shook hands.

"You're not coming with us?" I asked Uri.

"I'm afraid not. I have some things to tend to." He took my hand and placed a piece of folded-up paper into it. "Enjoy your tour. I will see you again very soon."

And with that, Dr. Uri Nevon left our company, proceeded down the marble steps of Saint Peter's Basilica, and disappeared into the throngs of people in the piazza.

CHAPTER FOUR

"Shall we continue inside?" Dr. Maderno asked me.

"Sure," I said, trying to hide my boredom and disappointment.

Dr. Maderno was an intelligent man with a noble pedigree who could no doubt teach me a lot about architecture, and I was certainly honored to be in his presence.

But he was no Uri.

Dr. Maderno had just finished giving me the history of the site of Saint Peter's Basilica. He'd explained that a simple shrine had been erected on this site in the second century, and the first basilica was commissioned by Constantine and completed around A.D. 349. After about a thousand years the basilica was crumbling, and the first stone of a new church was laid by Pope Julius II in 1506.

Over the ensuing decades, popes came and went, architects died and were replaced, and design schemes evolved. The current basilica and piazza as we see it today took more than a century and a half to build, and combines Renaissance and Baroque elements that form a shrine that is massive, masterful, and magnificent—if not bewildering.

Dr. Maderno knew architecture inside and out, and laid out all the facts, and could answer every one of my questions. But he lacked a certain amount of passion and excitement (not to mention brevity) that made me favor Uri as a teacher. Nothing personal, of course. I guess since Uri had been my most recent teacher of sorts, I automatically started favoring his style of instruction.

But I was still fascinated to hear about Bernini's saint-topped colonnade, and Michelangelo's dome, and Dr. Maderno's ancestor's decision to cave to papal pressure and create a palatial façade. And as the tour continued, I was starting to get the feeling the reason I was here had nothing to do with the exterior of Saint Peter's Basilica, and everything to do with what was inside. More specifically, what lay *underneath*.

Perhaps that's why Uri had insisted our journey start here. He was laying the groundwork for our next adventure, and it all started beneath our feet: the necropolis that housed popes and aristocrats and commoners and one very important martyr.

The man who received the keys to the kingdom from Jesus.

Saint Peter the Apostle.

I'd heard a rumor once that Saint Peter wasn't actually buried beneath Saint Peter's but in Jerusalem, the city of his birth. It was a rumor that didn't hold much water, but as I stood there listening to the professor speak, I thought what an interesting—and controversial—book that would make.

Perhaps Uri thought so too. Perhaps Saint Peter was the reason I was here.

And Perhaps Uri's note held the answer. It was currently burning a hole in my pocket, and the sooner I could get the tour over with, the sooner I could read it.

So when Dr. Maderno asked me to step inside, through the main entrance of the basilica, I couldn't resist the urge to take the conversation in a new direction—and speed the tour up a bit.

"Tell me about your ancestor, Carlo Maderno," I said, taking in the vast interior for the second time in a decade. I had forgotten how beautifully overwhelming it was, with its long stretch of nave and the soaring height of the dome and the hodge-podge of ornate design styles.

"You want to know about Carlo?" the professor said, motioning me to walk with him down the 620-foot nave.

"Certainly."

"But there is so much to see. The nave, the apse, the Treasury..." he pointed in the direction of each as we walked. "Così magnifico."

"I know it's all magnificent. I've been here before."

Dr. Maderno stopped and his eyes widened, as if shocked by this news. "Why didn't you say so, signora?"

"It's been a long time...and I'd forgotten a lot about this place."

"Time does have a way of robbing us of our memories," Dr. Maderno said, sighing. "So you are happy to be receiving a re-education?"

"Re-education. I like your choice of words. Yes, I'm thrilled."

"Rome is an excellent place for learning."

"I just wish I knew what I'm going to be learning..." I said, more to myself than to the professor. I scanned the ornately painted ceiling down the length of the nave, shielding my eyes from the shafts of sunlight pouring in from all directions.

I looked at the professor and he was grinning at me, letting me know he'd heard what I said. "Uri will let you know when the time is right," he said.

"Mm hmm," I said.

"Tell me, Miss Beltane. Are you upset that you're not being re-educated from Uri's perspective?"

I was taken aback by his brashness, and then I was worried I was giving off subtle clues of disappointment—and ungratefulness.

"Of course not," I said. "You are the only person I could envision guiding me. Thank you for taking the time."

"But up until an hour ago you didn't even know I existed. You thought you'd be receiving a tour from Uri."

"Well, you're an architecture professor, so I'd say you're the better authority."

The professor laughed and ran a hand through his gelled hair. "Perhaps, but I'm not as handsome or charming as Uri."

I wanted to know more about the Dr. Maderno's personal and professional life, and I certainly wanted to hear all the juicy bits of his familial history. But I couldn't deny that at that moment, I'd rather be standing in front of Uri.

"Who are you fooling?" I said, smirking. "I'm sure you're quite the lady's man."

The professor only smiled and I turned my attention back to my surroundings.

I could see the entrance to the necropolis just in front of me, a large semi-circular hole in the floor, and just behind it the Baldacchino, an extravagant stone canopy under which lays a plain slab of marble known as the Papal Altar. It is here where the Pope says mass, and it is deep beneath this altar where Christendom's very first pope is supposedly entombed.

I believed this was the reason Uri brought me to Rome—to explore the depths of the necropolis where the beloved Saint Peter supposedly lies.

When I turned my attention back to my tour guide, he was smiling at me in an all-knowing way, as if he could read my thoughts.

"You really don't know why you're here, signora?" the professor said, awakening me from my stupor.

"To research Rome and Saint Peter for my next book," I said. "That much I can guess."

His narrow-set hazel eyes probed mine, perhaps searching for the true answer.

I decided to give it to him, what I thought was the true answer. Yes, he was a stranger, but he was Uri's friend. I felt I could trust the company he kept. Plus, the professor had set time aside to meet me, and seemed to sympathize with whatever he felt was distracting me.

"I think I'm here to prove if Saint Peter is buried beneath the basilica that bears his name," I said.

Dr. Maderno shrank back from the revelation. "Oh."

Then I took a deep breath. "And I'm here to prove if Uri and I could have a relationship."

Dr. Maderno clapped his hands together, seeming to have already forgotten the implications of my first statement. "Of course!" he said. "Amore! You and Uri are in amore!"

"No, no, you misunderstand," I said, attempting to calm the professor from the sudden rapture that had overtaken him. He was nodding his head and gesticulating wildly with his hands, spouting phrases in Italian that only he could understand.

"I can't...I mean, I don't *love* Uri...and he doesn't *love* me," I said. "At least I don't think he does... Anyway, it's complicated."

The professor composed himself. "I understand," he said, his toothy grin melting into a smile. He took a step forward and raised his index finger as if to prove a point. "I saw the way he looked at you, and the way you looked at him. *Gli occhi dicono tutto.* The eyes tell all."

I blushed and said nothing.

"Okay, Miss Beltane," the professor said. "Tour's over."

"What? But I want you to re-educate me about Saint Peter's."

"There's nothing left for me to show you. The one thing that remains, your reason for being here...Uri will have to show you."

As we made our way back down the long nave to the front entrance, I realized I had underestimated the professor. While Giovanni Maderno the professor was staid and somewhat boring, Giovanni Maderno the man was intuitive and sympathetic and full of life.

"I truly want to know about your ancestor Carlo," I said, emerging into the brightness of the piazza.

"When you are ready, I will be here," the professor said, shaking my hand. He gave me a quick bow and walked off in the same direction from whence he came.

There was one last thing for me to do before heading back to the hotel room.

Walking through the piazza, past flocks of birds and groups of tourists, and with stone saints as my witnesses, I opened Uri's note.

Dearest Mara,

I felt a thorough and proper tour of Saint Peter's Basilica with just Giovanni was in order for you to gain a frame of reference for the rest of our adventure. As Renaissance architecture is not my forte, I felt it best to leave you in the hands of someone who is not only an expert in the field, but also a trusted colleague. I hope that after meeting Giovanni and seeing the basilica, you agree with my decision.

I imagine you are feeling impatient for the next part of our adventure to begin. But trust me when I say there is much to do first...

Please meet me for dinner tonight at 8 p.m. at La Gallina Bianca. We will discuss, among other things, the cities that will unlock the key to your next mystery...

To our next adventure,

Uri

CHAPTER FIVE

Later that evening I found myself waiting for the subway at Stazione Termini, Rome's central transportation station. From here you can get to any part of the city by subway, bus, or taxi. I was re-reading Uri's note for the fifth or sixth time.

The note mentioned cities. As in, more than one...

Traveling to multiple cities during this trip was something I definitely hadn't anticipated, but I should have. I was dealing with Uri, after all. I refolded the note and put it back into my purse as the train pulled into the station. I deboarded at the stop closest to La Gallina Bianca, the restaurant where Uri had requested I meet him for dinner, and soaked up my surroundings, such as they were, during the brief walk to the restaurant.

Aside from a museum or two and the Santa Maria Maggiore, one of the great Roman basilicas, this part of town was mostly hotels and restaurants. So while it attracted large groups of tourists for its good eats and sound accommodations, the buildings were hardly ancient.

But the area was still buzzing.

I continued walking southwest down Via Cavour, a wide street and main artery that led out of Stazione Termini. Cars and mopeds rushed by in a blur of noise and light, business men and women whipped passed me in a rush chirping away on cell phones, and lovers strolled arm and arm seemingly in no hurry at all. It was 7:30 p.m., the air was warm with a slight breeze, and Roman nightlife was starting to get underway.

Thomas and I hadn't visited this part of town, preferring instead to stay centrally located in the heart of ancient Rome. So this was a new experience to me which, combined with the uncertainty of my visit with Uri and a growling stomach, was causing a lightheadedness that food could only partially solve.

There were a few tables outside La Gallina Bianca under an awning, which is where I spotted Uri, sipping a glass of red wine.

Our eyes locked and Uri smiled, lowering his glass and standing to greet me. I could feel my cheeks starting to flush, and I hadn't even had any wine yet.

"You look wonderful," Uri said, motioning for me to sit down. "Wine?"

There was an empty glass sitting in front of me and a wine bottle perched on the edge of the table. As I sat down I realized it was more of a statement than a question, because Uri had poured me a glass of wine before I'd had a chance to respond or even get comfortable.

"Wine is not as popular in Jerusalem as it once was," Uri was saying as I settled in. "So I enjoy coming to a country where it flows freely."

"Isn't that ironic?" I said, taking a sip and hoping it would start to calm my nerves. "The fact that wine is synonymous with Jesus and the Holy Land and has now lost its popularity in that part of the world."

"Hmmm...yes," Uri said, furrowing his brow in contemplation. "The most mentioned beverage in the bible—and the principle alcoholic beverage of the ancient Israelites—has now lost out to vodka as the most widely consumed alcoholic beverage by modern-day Israelis."

"Wine is the most mentioned beverage in the bible?"

"Over two hundred times," Uri said. "But what we would call wine today referred to many types of drinks in biblical times, both alcoholic and non-alcoholic."

"Really?" I said. Then I raised my glass. "Well, I'll drink to that."

Uri laughed and we clinked our glasses together.

A light breeze sent a chill through me as I took the sip of wine, and goose bumps emerged on my bare arms and legs. I draped a sweater around my shoulders, glancing at Uri's attire. He was wearing what I would call normal clothing for a university professor: gray khakis, light-blue button-up oxford shirt, and a black corduroy blazer. Not unlike what he wore the first time we had a meal together.

It was two years ago in Jerusalem, and we were meeting for lunch at an outdoor café. He was to tell me what he knew about the Talpiot tomb, and I was to use that knowledge for the novel that would become my first runaway best-seller. We were strangers with a similar interest, nothing more, nothing less. My brown khakis and pull-over collared shirt said professional and climate-appropriate for an alfresco lunch meeting in June, and was completely acceptable for what I thought would be a one-time meeting. What I had worn meant nothing because I thought I'd never see him again.

Turns out, Uri and I had been by each other's side for days on end, spent time in each other's atmospheres, gotten to know each other on a personal level. Saw our faults and strengths and weaknesses. Shared a jail cell...and an intimate moment that I simultaneously hoped would never end and wished had never happened...

Uri and I had history now, and it couldn't be ignored.

So now, more then ever, and especially after a two-year absence, I thought my choice of wardrobe for this dinner meeting was important. It would speak more about my intentions, and how I felt. I thought a dress would convey that I was interested in Uri on more than just a professional level. I wanted to seem available but not desperate, sexy but not slutty, curious but not neurotic about his feelings for me.

Who knew that swaths of cotton could carry so much weight?

"Everything all right?" Uri asked, eyeing me curiously.

"Of course," I said. "Just wondering what you have in store next."

"Ah, yes," Uri said, that familiar twinkle in his eye. He motioned to our waiter. "But first things first. First, we eat."

• • • •

HALF AN HOUR LATER, Uri and I were finishing a thin-crust pizza and drinking the last sips of the bottle of wine. My stomach was full but still uneasy, and my head was buzzing from alcohol and a thousand thoughts that were running through my mind. We hadn't said much of substance, mostly small talk and normal conversation pleasantries.

"So," Uri said, dabbing his mouth with a napkin and placing in on his plate. "What do you think of Rome so far?"

"Just as I remember it."

"I didn't know you'd been to Rome before."

"Long time ago," I said. "Honeymoon...me and Thomas."

"Ah," Uri said, looking down at the table. He cleared his throat but remained silent. If he was wondering how Thomas was doing, if I still saw or spoke to him, he didn't ask. And I didn't say.

It hardly mattered anyway. Thomas was now happily remarried to a woman he'd met at work. A few weeks before I left for Rome, my best friend Lisa informed me that his new wife had given birth to their first child, a son named Samuel.

I was happy for Thomas, for finally getting what he'd wanted, what he never would've gotten from me—children, a family, fatherhood.

I mailed the happy couple a blue onesie with giraffes on it, along with my congratulations on a card signed only, "M." I was hoping that by doing so, Thomas would affectionately remember how we used to sign notes to each other using only the first letter of our name. I was hoping he'd see it as a sign of peace, that I was okay and had moved on, and that he was okay and not harboring any regrets about our time together.

The thank-you card I received in the mail a week later was signed "Christina and T."

I cried for hours that day—out of joy, out of pity, out of relief.

The next day I received an email from Uri, inviting me to Rome...

So while I wasn't completely over Thomas, the days of M and T were over, and dispatching unresolved feelings for an ex-husband on the man sitting across from me—a man I hoped would become a more permanent part of my future—would do little to increase whatever affection he had for me. Not to mention make both of us rather uncomfortable. Which is why I didn't bring up Ziva, although naturally I was dying to know if the days of Ziva and Uri were similarly over. I wasn't ready to know the truth yet. I wanted to enjoy this time alone with Uri.

"Did you enjoy your tour of Saint Peter's with Giovanni?" Uri finally said.

I sighed, glad that the topic of exes had been successfully avoided.

"It was...interesting."

It was then that I started to feel the effects of four glasses of wine. My head was light and dizzy, as if at any moment it would pop off my neck and float away like a balloon into the Roman night. I gulped down half a glass of water, attempting to counteract the alcohol swirling around in my veins.

A piece of pizza crust lay discarded on my plate. I picked it up and bit into it, hoping even the slightest bit of bread would help curb the intoxication that was assaulting my system.

"He's very knowledgeable," Uri was saying as I was gulping down the last of my water.

"I'll say," I said with a slight giggle.

"Mara," Uri said, ignoring or perhaps not sensing the hidden meaning in my last comment. "I think he'll be great for your book. His knowledge, his experience...it's just want you need."

"*You're* what I need," I said, foolishly, drunkenly, in a half-whisper. I was still holding the glass of water to my mouth.

Uri leaned forward. "What?"

I froze, the glass still in my hand, my eyes wide with embarrassment.

"I didn't hear what you said," Uri said.

I put the glass down and attempted to compose myself. "What I need is... for you to confirm my suspicion as to why I'm in Rome."

"And your suspicion is....?"

I paused, contemplating my next move. Should I confront Uri and his intentions?

He had drunk just as much wine as me. Surely he was under the influence and his altered state would allow me to extract his true feelings for me. Perhaps he could be compromised into telling the truth.

But I decided to play it safe. For now.

"Saint Peter," I said.

Uri smiled. "What about him?"

"Perhaps he's not buried in Rome after all..."

Uri raised an eyebrow and I knew I was getting warmer.

I continued. "Perhaps he's buried in Jerusalem, the place of his birth. You want us to find out if that is at all possible. And you think that should be the subject of my next novel."

Uri reached across the table and took my hand. "Mara yakiri," he said. *My dear Mara.* "You have hit the nail on the head. But you must know by now that it isn't as easy as that."

"What do you mean?

Uri drained the final sips of wine from his glass. "Lev will lead the way."

"Lev? What's he got to do with this...?"

Uri was quiet a moment. He folded his hands in his lap and smiled at me, as if waiting for me to guess.

"Is Lev in Rome?" I asked, excited that I might get to see the young man who was just as responsible for the success of my novel as Uri was.

"No, Lev is in Jerusalem. Where he's always been."

I was drunk on wine and want, and more confused than ever. If only he would tell me what was going on—inside his head, inside his heart, beneath the city of Rome.

"I don't understand," I said.

"Don't get too comfortable in Rome," he said, leaning across the table with the familiar twinkle in his eye.

Immediately my stomach lurched, knowing that Dr. Uri Nevon had something up his sleeve. He always did.

"Okay," I said cautiously. "Why?"

"If we want to find out if Saint Peter is buried in Jerusalem, then we must go to Jerusalem. Pack a bag, we leave tomorrow."

CHAPTER SIX

I stepped out of the heat into the air conditioned store. Uri walked in after me, the bell above the door announcing our arrival. We both paused, waiting for the shopkeeper to emerge. Looking around, I could see nothing had changed: same midnight blue carpet, same white walls, same glass display cases in the middle of the store.

The store clerk emerged from behind the blue-curtained door and stopped short when he saw us.

"Miss Mara!" he said, rushing up to me. He threw his arms around me and gave a quick squeeze.

"Hi, Lev," I said.

"Welcome back to Jerusalem."

"Thank you."

Lev Geller hadn't changed much. He'd ditched his glasses for contacts, but otherwise, he had the same deep voice of a man, the same lanky frame of an adolescent, and the same smooth face of a boy.

"Dr. Nevon," Lev said, shaking hands with Uri.

"Hello, young man."

"You were expecting us, right?" I asked Lev, looking to Uri for confirmation. Uri nodded.

"Yes. Dr. Nevon paid me a visit last week and let me know. I was so excited! So much to catch up on! Your bestseller and my new girlfriend and Dr. Nevon's news and of course your reason for coming back to Jerusalem..."

"Wait," I said, looking at Uri. "What news?"

"You didn't tell Miss Mara your news?" Lev asked.

"Not yet," Uri said, eyeing Lev. "There will be time for that."

"Sorry, professor. I hope I haven't spoiled the surprise."

"It's fine."

Uri and Lev always had a way of carrying on a conversation as if I wasn't even present.

"Hello!" I said. "What surprise? What's going on?"

Uri turned to me. "There's something I need to tell you that doesn't involve your reason for being here."

My heart was hammering in my chest. "What is it?"

"Not here. Not now," Uri said.

I sighed heavily. "When?"

"Soon. I will tell you very soon. I promise. We have business to take care of first."

"Fine," I said, smiling weakly at Uri and then at Lev. "Where do we start?"

• • • •

I TRIED TO PUSH THOUGHTS of Uri's "news" from my head as the plan came together, but it was useless. It was all I could think of. Why did Lev have to say anything? Whatever it was, why hadn't Uri told me at dinner the other night? He'd had the perfect opportunity.

"The tomb of Saint Peter, huh....?" Lev was saying when I snapped to and mentally rejoined the conversation. "That's bound to be another best-seller."

The three of us were in the back room of Lev's store, sitting on folding chairs. We sat close together, our knees almost touching, our voices hushed. It was as if we were a secret society planning a hostile take-over.

"We'll see..." I said.

"So what help do you need from me?" Lev asked, looking in turn at both of us.

I shrugged and motioned to Uri. "Talk to him. He's the man with the plan."

We both looked at Uri.

"We need to get inside the Church of the Flagellation," Uri said flatly.

"That's easy enough," Lev said. "It's open to the pubic."

Uri shook his head. "We need to see an area that is...*off-limits*...to the public."

"I'm not understanding you, professor," Lev said.

"Have you heard of the Franciscan Custody of the Holy Land?"

"Sure. They're the friars who oversee the religious shrines of the Holy Land, including the Church of the Holy Sepulchre."

"And the Church of the Flagellation," Uri added.

"What about the Franciscans?" Lev asked.

"Yes, where are you going with this, Uri?" I asked.

Uri leaned in. "The Franciscans are in possession of ossuary shards rumored to be the bone box of none other than Saint Peter."

"I've heard that rumor," Lev said.

"I haven't," I said, hoping my statement would be a hint that Uri should explain more about the Franciscans, and what his plan was. But it proved fruitless, as Uri and Lev continued on with yet another private conversation like I wasn't even in the room.

"The ossuary shards are said to be housed somewhere within the Church of the Flagellation," Uri said, "and we need to see them."

"Good luck with that," Lev said. "If the rumor's true, you can bet the friars have them hidden away somewhere, away from the public, out of site."

"We must talk to someone about them," Uri said. "Can you help us?"

Lev looked uneasy. "I...I don't know, professor..."

"That's a pretty tall order, Uri," I finally interjected. "I mean, if these Franciscan people are as secretive as most religious organizations..."

"You have no idea," Uri whispered.

Lev and I looked at each other.

"What do you mean?" I asked.

"Never mind, never mind," Uri said, waving his hand in the air as if wiping a smudge from a pane of glass. "It doesn't matter."

"Does the Vatican know that this Franciscan organization is in possession of an ossuary they claim belongs to Saint Peter?" I asked. "Because, you know, the very existence of this ossuary could be considered sacrilege."

"Of course the Vatican knows," Uri said. "Who do you think entrusted them with the secret? The Vatican entrusts *many* secrets to the Franciscans."

"Oh, *really*?" I said, suddenly more interested than ever in this secret society and their connection to the Vatican. It could mean many more book ideas...

"As you can imagine," Uri continued, "it is very difficult to get anyone to comment on such controversial things, let alone Church officials. Which is why we must consider *every* resource available to us." Then Uri turned to Lev, as if prompting him to action.

"Professor, I'd love to help you," Lev said, "but I'm afraid my only connections are within the Jerusalem police and the Israeli Antiquities Authority."

"Yes, yes, I know," Uri said, more to himself than to Lev. His head was tilted up, as if the answer to our dilemma was written on the ceiling. "I've befriended a lot of people in my years as a college professor, but not many members of religious organizations. Certainly not any high-ranking ones with the power to help us."

"Well, you did break into the Talpiot tomb—twice," I said, attempting to lighten the mood. "I think you can forget about becoming BFFs with any Vatican insiders."

Uri seemed to ignore me, lost in his own thoughts, and Lev only scrunched his face at me. "What's a BFF?" he asked.

I shook my head at him. "Don't worry about it."

"Oh, okay," he replied, still looking befuddled. Then his face changed. "What about Ziva?"

At the mention of Lev's sister, Uri's head snapped up—and my heart leapt in my chest.

"What about her?" Uri said.

"Well, I know she hasn't worked for the IAA for awhile, but perhaps—"

"She's fallen out of favor with the IAA," Uri said, rather curtly.

Among other things, the Israel Antiquities Authority, or IAA, is in charge of the excavation, preservation, and conservation of the country's ancient treasures. That includes the Talpiot tomb—the controversial first-century burial cave rumored to be the lost tomb of Jesus, and the subject of my polarizing best-selling thriller. Lev's sister once worked for the IAA as an archeologist. She and Uri were engaged at one time, but she broke up with him because she felt his obsession with the Talpiot tomb would always trump their relationship.

Regardless, she used her power and authority within the IAA to help Uri and Lev break into the tomb, a decision that got her fired. Uri felt responsible that Ziva lost a job she loved, so he helped her get a teaching position at Hebrew University, where he was a professor.

During my first visit to Jerusalem to research the Talpiot tomb for my novel, I'd met several IAA members, all of whom, while nice, were guarded in their opinions of the legitimacy of the first-century burial cave being the final resting place of Jesus. None of them agreed to help me, and none would come forth with personal opinions of the Talpiot tomb. And rightfully so. Their job is to protect and preserve the cultural heritage of their country, not spout off egregious statements about unproven Jesus family history.

So in the end, it wasn't the IAA who helped me fulfill my quest of gaining entrance to the Talpiot tomb, but a religious scholar, a young Israeli boy...and a member of the Jerusalem police.

The chief of police, to be exact.

As his face flashed in my mind's eye, I quickly dismissed Lev's idea. Why would Ziva Feldman, a woman with no ties left to the IAA, and who had gotten fired from her job because of her involvement with the tomb break-in, agree to help us? Besides, hadn't she moved on with her life? Forgotten all about Uri and married another man?

The chief of police, to be exact?

His face flashed in front of me again, along with an idea. And it didn't involve the woman who had broken Uri's heart.

Rather, it involved her husband.

"What about Benjamin?" I asked. "He's still the Jerusalem police chief, right? What do you think, Lev? Think your brother-in-law would help us again?"

Lev looked at Uri, as if waiting to see his reaction before responding.

"What are you thinking, Mara?" Uri said.

"Maybe Benjamin could say he needs complete access to the Church of the Flagellation for some police matter?"

"Why would he agree to help us?" Uri asked. "What's in it for him?"

I shrugged.

"Wouldn't the friars see right through that?" Lev asked.

I knew I was grasping at straws. The ridiculousness of the idea was made apparent by the look of incredulity on Lev's face and Uri's blank stare.

"Sorry," I said. "It was the only thing I could think of."

"I guess I could ask him..." Lev said.

Uri's face was still devoid of any emotion. Finally, he said, "I'll give you twenty-four hours, Lev. Get us in to see the hidden ossuary shards of Saint Peter." Then, turning to me, he said, "Do you remember our time spent on the Mount of Olives?"

"Of course," I said. "You can't discuss Jesus' time in Jerusalem without mentioning the Mount of Olives. And it was one of the highlights on my first trip."

"Wonderful," Uri said, clapping his hands together. "We shall visit tomorrow."

"I didn't realize I hadn't seen it all the first time."

"Oh, there's much more to learn, my dear Mara," Uri said, a twinkle in his eye. "And be sure to wear comfortable shoes. We will literally be following in the footsteps of Jesus, and it's not an easy trek."

CHAPTER SEVEN

We stood on top of the Mount of Olives, the walls of the Old City of Jerusalem down to our right, and the Valley of Jehoshaphat below us. Rows of sand-colored stone tombs spread out in front of us, numbering in the thousands, evidence that millennia of Jews believed this to be the place where the dead would be resurrected on the Day of Judgment. Christians and Muslims hold this same belief, so the valley is dotted with the cemeteries of three major faiths.

From atop the Mount of Olives, I could see it all: the whole Kidron Valley, or Valley of Jehoshaphat; Mount Zion across the valley, the hill synonymous with biblical times and the final days of Jesus; and the Dome of the Rock off in the distance, its gold dome a shining beacon proclaiming the glory of Jerusalem.

We were making our way down the mountain to Dominus Flevit, a chapel built in 1955 on the spot where medieval pilgrims said Jesus sat and wept over the fate of Jerusalem. The name Dominus Flevit, in fact, is Latin for "The Lord Wept," and the building is shaped like a teardrop to further symbolize Jesus' association with this land.

The Franciscan Custody of the Holy Land, the society of friars Uri had mentioned the day before in Lev's store, had commissioned the chapel, and to this day hold it in their trust.

Uri and I were here to see what was discovered while the foundation was being dug: an ancient necropolis containing ossuaries, one of which was very rare...

An ossuary inscribed with the name Simon bar Jonah.

Simon, son of Jonah.

No other ossuary in existence is inscribed with this name, making it very rare. No remains—human or otherwise—were found inside the ossuary and the bone box itself mysteriously disappeared, but fragments remain. Fragments that Uri thought were being hidden by the Franciscan Custody of the Holy Land inside the Church of the Flagellation.

Since Saint Peter's name was originally Simon, some believe the Simon bar Jonah ossuary belonged to this venerated saint, which explains why the remaining fragments would be hidden away, out of sight and out of mind. Authenticating a stone box found in Jerusalem to be that of the prince of the apostles, Christendom's first pope, would upend the Catholic Church's agenda, negate the tradition of Saint Peter's martyrdom and burial in Rome...and possibly start a holy war.

It was Lev's job to get us inside the Church of the Flagellation to see the ossuary shards, a seemingly impossible task, I thought, as we approached the courtyard of the Dominus Flevit chapel.

"So where is the necropolis?" I asked, returning my thoughts to the matter at hand. I shielded my eyes from the blazing sun and looked around for an entrance to the underground world of the dead that was discovered during this site's excavation in the mid-20th century.

"There are burial caves all around us," Uri said. "The one I want to show you is there." He pointed to the far side of the church and led me to an open cave carved in rock. Inside the cave were dozens of ossuaries, scattered on the stone floor and resting inside carved recesses. Some of the bone boxes were ornately carved, some were simple and plain. Some were complete with lids intact, others had lids that were cracked or broken or missing altogether.

"The Simon bar Jonah ossuary was found in here," Uri said, carefully navigating around the cave so as to not disturb the ossuaries that littered the stone floor. "Along with ossuaries bearing the names Mary, Martha, and Lazarus."

"So the fact that ossuaries were found here dates this particular cave to the early first century, during the time period that ossuaries were a popular medium for the storage of remains," I said. "Which means the people buried here most probably knew or had heard of Jesus."

"Or were early followers of Jesus," Uri added.

"That would make a lot of sense, since if I'm not mistaken the Mount of Olives was a popular meeting place for Jesus and his disciples."

"Yes. Not only that, but the Bible prophesizes that Jesus will stand on the Mount of Olives upon his return to Earth."

"So naturally, early Christians and followers of Jesus would want to be buried here, on the Mount, closer to where Jesus is said to return." I paused, suddenly realizing the true importance of where I stood. "Making this as good a place as any to find Peter."

Uri smiled and nodded, and I felt good about our progress so far. I felt like we had already made headway proving that Saint Peter might have been buried here, in Jerusalem, in a cave near where Jesus is said to have spent some of his most positive days as preacher.

And it felt good to be in Uri's presence, to soak in his enthusiasm. At moments like this, I was more than just a simple American girl from Philadelphia and he a learned Israeli academic. We were intellectual equals, worthy and capable research partners, and possible compatible life mates. It made for an equal balance of power, strength and smarts that made us an unstoppable team.

"Let's not forget something else," Uri said, waking me from my romantic notion.

I looked up and met Uri's hazel eyes and noticed he was looking at me in that curious way of his: eyebrows arched and mouth set, as if willing me to guess what was on his mind.

I shrugged and admitted that I knew of no other evidence suggesting Peter's burial in Jerusalem.

"There is no record anywhere in the New Testament of Peter traveling to Rome," Uri said, sitting down on the edge of a large chunk of rock. "The New Testament! Supposedly the most accurate and detailed account of Jesus and his disciples, and it says nothing about Peter being in Rome. It mentions his travels to Lydda and Joppa and Jerusalem, but nothing about Rome."

"You're right," I said, suddenly remembering that the New Testament also doesn't mention that Peter was the first pope. I sat down opposite Uri, on a low masonry wall. "Surely the writers of the New Testament would've mentioned Peter's travels to and from Rome had they happened, right?"

"You'd think so. But do you want to hear something even more interesting? Even Peter himself is silent on his whereabouts."

"What do you mean?"

"His own writings are words of wisdom and rules to live by but never mention his travels. Paul mentions meeting up with Peter in various places throughout Judea, and Paul said he himself traveled to Rome. But Paul never mentions seeing or meeting up with Peter in Rome."

"If this is true, if Peter never set foot in Rome, why would Constantine and the Catholic Church choose Rome as the place to build a monument to venerate him?"

"That's the big question" Uri said, shifting positions on his rock seat. "Peter was considered 'The Apostle to the Jews'. So what possible motivation is there for the Catholic Church to perpetuate the notion that he was martyred and buried in Rome? That, my dear Mara, is the heart of the issue."

We were silent for a moment, Uri assumedly allowing the weight of the issue to take shape in my brain.

Suddenly, he jumped up and motioned for me to follow him to the back corner of the cave. I left my perch on the low masonry wall and slowly jockeyed around the myriad of ossuaries that littered my path, as if navigating a minefield.

Uri crouched down next to a plain ossuary on the floor. "Remember that there are two sides to every argument," he said. "We've just discussed the evidence we have placing Peter's burial in Jerusalem. Here's the argument *against* Peter's burial in Jerusalem." He tilted the bone box up in my direction, making sure the lid didn't slide off. When he did that I noticed an upside down V symbol on the shorter side of the ossuary and a matching symbol on the edge of the lid. Each upside down V had a small circle in the middle. Uri traced both Vs with a dusty finger.

I had seen this V symbol, or chevron, before.

A similar symbol, though much larger, marks the opening of the Talpiot tomb.

"Chevrons," I said, and Uri smiled.

"What do you know about chevrons?" he asked.

"The same symbol appears in larger scale at the entrance of the Talpiot tomb."

Uri's eyes narrowed. "Are you sure about that?"

"I was until just now."

Uri laughed, then traced both the V symbols again with his finger. "Two Vs are etched on the supposed ossuary of Saint Peter, as well. One on the box and one on the lid."

"There you go!" I said, crouching down alongside Uri. "All the symbols match. Chevrons on the Saint Peter bone box and a chevron etched at the entrance to the Talpiot tomb. Surely there's a connection..."

Uri stayed silent, allowing me to work it out in my mind.

"The Talpiot tomb is rumored to be the final resting place of Jesus and his family members, and there's a chevron marking the entrance. The Simon bar Jonah ossuary is rumored to belong to Saint Peter, and there are chevrons etched on it. It helps cement the idea that they all knew each other, hung out together, preached together.... in Jerusalem."

I knew my statement sounded far-fetched, and it was confirmed when Uri started shaking his head at me.

"The chevrons don't match," he said. "The Vs on the Simon bar Jonah ossuary and the larger one on the Talpiot tomb..."

"Okay, they don't match *exactly*," I said, not ready to give up my argument just yet. "But I remember you saying that the chevron symbol pre-dates Christianity..."

Uri shifted positions, taking a seat on a small outcropping of rock. I sat opposite him.

"Ah, so you remember something *else* about chevrons?" he asked, as if my current line of thinking was what he was aiming for all along.

"Yes, that the chevron symbol is possibly Jewish in origin."

Uri smirked at me. "Go on."

"The Talpiot tomb was most certainly the resting place of an early first-century Jewish family, which would explain the chevron etched at the entrance."

"And?"

"And we know that Peter was Jewish, which could explain the presence of chevrons on his ossuary."

"You are correct, but..."

"But what? You just helped me prove my theory."

"You are correct only to a point," Uri said.

"What do you mean?"

"It's true that the chevron is possibly a Jewish symbol, and that Peter was Jewish, and that the family buried in the Talpiot tomb—whoever they were—were most likely Jewish..."

I sighed, knowing that another but was coming. "But...?"

"But, the chevrons on the ossuaries and the large one marking the entrance to the Talpiot tomb aren't used in the same way," Uri said. "They don't have the same meaning. Each one depicts something different."

"It's the 'mason's mark' argument, isn't it?" I said, referring to how stone masons regularly carved symbols onto the ossuaries they created in order to denote how the box and lid were supposed to line up.

"Yes, exactly," Uri said. "The chevrons on the Simon bar Jonah ossuary—and this ossuary, as well—were meant to show lid and box alignment."

"So what about the chevron at the entrance of the Talpiot tomb?"

Uri shrugged. "Who knows? The chevron, or gable in its most simple form, was a popular motif in the first century A.D. This artistic design could be found everywhere—carved into buildings, depicted on currency, most certainly used as a simple way for stone masons to mark their work...and as a way to denote the entrance to a tomb."

"What are you trying to say?"

"That the Talpiot tomb chevron is still a mystery. It could've been used as a way to denote that a Jewish family was buried there. But more than likely, the etching is meant to symbolize a gable, or roof. Meaning something or someone is housed there."

"So my theory that the presence of chevrons connects the Talpiot tomb and the Simon bar Jonah ossuary is crap."

"I wouldn't put it so harshly," Uri said, "but it does make it harder to prove that the bone box in question belongs to Saint Peter."

"It would be like suggesting the Apple logo, one of the most recognizable brands of the 20th century, etched onto a tombstone denoted the final resting place of Steve Jobs."

Uri laughed at my common-day reference. "Yes, something like that."

"So it makes getting into the Church of the Flagellation, and seeing those ossuary shards, all the more important."

Uri nodded. "There's not much left of the ossuary, but what remains could be the key to solving the mystery."

"Hard to believe that a simple group of friars is what stands between us and the truth."

Suddenly Uri was on his feet, approaching where I sat. "These are not ordinary men and women," he said sternly, looking me dead in the eye.

"How so?" I asked, simultaneously intrigued and frightened by Uri's statement.

As is typical with Uri, he answered my question with a question.

"How are you feeling?"

"Honestly? Exhausted."

"Your physical strength will return," he said, placing his hands on my shoulders. "But be forewarned about tomorrow. You will need a different type of strength."

"What's tomorrow?"

"We will attempt to extract secrets."

"Secrets from whom?"

"The Ordo Fratrum Minorum."

"Who the heck are they?"

"No more questions today," Uri said, helping me to my feet. "Save your questions for tomorrow, when your mind is fresher."

"Okay. What exactly will I need a fresh mind for?"

"A battle of wills that will push the limits of your emotional endurance."

CHAPTER EIGHT

The Franciscan Custody of the Holy Land is a group of 300 friars and 100 "sisters," as their female counterparts are called, responsible for serving Christian shrines throughout the Holy Land. Funded by the Vatican, this group of "custodians," part of the Franciscan order, is in charge of almost eighty religious shrines and sanctuaries throughout Israel, Palestine, Jordan, Syria, Egypt, Lebanon, Cyprus and Rhodes. Some of the more famous and heavily visited sites in their charge include the Basilica of the Nativity in Bethlehem; the Basilica of the Annunciation in Nazareth; the Church of the Holy Sepulchre in Jerusalem; and the Church of the Flagellation, where I was headed with Uri at my side. We were hoping to see the supposed ossuary of Saint Peter. Or rather, the few fragments that remained.

Walking down a narrow cobbled alleyway through the Muslim Quarter within the walls of the Old City, I wondered how such a controversial object could be kept in plain site, yet remain such a secret. If the Church of the Flagellation was open to the public, then certainly thousands, if not millions, of people have viewed the ossuary shards. Unless they weren't on display. Perhaps they were hidden within the bowels of the complex, as Lev had suggested, out of sight and out of mind. That's what Uri and I were here to find out.

We approached the complex, which includes two chapels and a museum, turned right through a doorway and came across a small, glass-encased enclosure a few feet to our left. The door to the enclosure was propped open. A casually-dressed middle-aged man sat behind a small desk, reading a magazine. To our right was a small courtyard with vine-covered archways.

"So what's the plan?" I whispered to Uri and we approached the glass enclosure.

Uri had been mum on how the day would play out, which wasn't like him at all. He always had a plan, some details of which he chose to share so that I could plan accordingly, and other details he kept secret in order to surprise me. But this felt different. Uri had texted me the night before, something he usually didn't do, and asked me to meet him at Saint Stephen's Gate at 9 a.m. the next morning. No further instructions were given. And he hadn't spoken much during the walk to the Church of the Flagellation. The look on his face during our periods of silence suggested uncertainty and anxiety.

I was walking into this situation blindly, and, judging by the beads of sweat glistening on Uri's forehead, I had a feeling he was, too.

"Just follow my lead," he finally said, looking straight ahead.

The man inside the glass enclosure looked up from his magazine as we approached. Uri exchanged a few words in Hebrew with the man, who turned his back to us and reached for the phone.

"What's going on?" I whispered.

"Not sure yet," Uri said, keeping his eyes on the man as he whispered into the phone.

"What did you tell him?"

"I said we were here on official business for a guided tour and needed to speak with the head Father, the Franciscan in charge of this facility."

"What sort of official business did you say we were on?"

"I was vague about that part. But I did say we had an appointment."

The man hung up the phone and turned to face us. He said something to Uri in Hebrew.

I leaned over and whispered to Uri, "What did he say?"

The man's eyes slid to me. His lips were pulled tight and his eyes narrowed. "I said, Father Rossi, the head Father, is not available."

"Oh," I said, shrinking back from the glass a step. "But...but we had an appointment."

Uri put his right hand on the small of my back. That usually meant he wanted to take the lead and do all the talking.

The man noticed Uri's subtle movement and glared at each of us in turn. "Who or what did you say you represented?"

Uri was silent a moment as his eyes stayed peeled on the man behind the glass. "Let me explain..." he finally said, returning his arm to his side.

"Hebrew University!" I blurted out, unable to bear the tension any longer.

Uri turned suddenly in my direction, and the man behind the glass looked at me in confusion. My hand shot to my mouth.

"Excuse me, Miss?" the guard said.

"Well, you see, I am a...graduate student...at Hebrew University," I explained. "History major. Emphasis on biblical archeology." I pointed to Uri. "He's my...professor." My heart starting to thud. I was unsure if this was the right direction to take the conversation, if this was the direction Uri was going to go. But given how slow Uri's plan was taking, I thought my sudden plan was a better one...and much faster.

I would apologize to Uri later for my impetuousness.

The guard looked at Uri for affirmation. Uri nodded.

"We're here to see the Studium Museum and thought maybe a private tour could be arranged," I said, hoping to further ease his mind.

"It's true," Uri said matter-of-factly.

The guard's eyes darted back and forth between the two of us. Then he turned to Uri and said something to him in Hebrew.

"My apologies," Uri replied in English, no doubt for my benefit. "Certainly I should have known that the curator of the museum, not the head of the whole facility, gives tours." He laughed uneasily. "So silly of me. How could I not know? The curator and I are familiar with each other."

It was my turn to look at Uri in surprise. The guard's eyes narrowed again.

"I need to see credentials," he said. "Both of you."

My heart started pounding harder, realizing that this could be where the trail ended.

Uri pulled out his wallet and handed him a Hebrew University issued photo I.D. card. The guard looked it over closely.

"Professor Uri Nevon," he said. "Why does that name sound familiar?" The guard looked up at Uri, his eyes still narrowed in disbelief.

Uri was silent for a moment, then glanced down at the magazine the guard had been reading when we arrived. It was open to an article about the ongoing Israeli and Palestinian conflict.

"Perhaps you've read one of the five history books I've written?" Uri said.

The guard glared at Uri a moment. "Perhaps," he said, handing the I.D. card back. Then he turned his attention to me. "Miss? I.D. please."

"I don't have a student I.D.," I said, hoping he'd let me slide.

"Passport? Driver's license?"

I reached into my bag, pulled out my passport and handed it to the guard. Panic was setting in.

He flipped through the pages. "You're an American studying abroad?"

I cleared my throat. "Yes."

"Where's your student visa?" he asked. "You need a visa to study in Israel."

"I...I...I..." I was at a complete loss for words.

And I had a feeling this was the end of the road. I had blown our chance to see the supposed Saint Peter ossuary. Proving the ossuary belonged to Saint Peter was crucial to my making the case that he was buried in Jerusalem and not Rome, as tradition has long held. Without that piece of the puzzle, there would be no novel.

I didn't dare look at Uri. I couldn't bear to see the look of disappointment that must certainly be on his face.

"She's not going to be in Jerusalem long enough to need a student visa," Uri suddenly said.

I looked up and the guard was glaring at Uri.

"What?" the guard said.

"She has obtained special permission from Hebrew University to study for only half a semester, one and a half months, for which she only needs a tourist visa."

Finally I looked at Uri, at his handsome profile, and the renewed sparkle in his eyes.

The guard turned his attention back to my passport, flipping through the pages again. As he did, Uri turned to me and winked.

I smiled and breathed a sigh of relief and was even happier when the guard found the Israeli stamp on my passport. Satisfied, the guard handed my passport back to me with what sounded like a sigh of defeat.

"I've taken the liberty of alerting the curator that you are here," he announced.

"What?" Uri said, alarmed. "That's not necessary. We don't wish to bother her. We can walk around ourselves."

It was then I realized Uri had lied about his relationship with the curator of the Studium Museum. And that the guard must have made *two* phone calls while his back was turned to us.

"No trouble at all, professor," the guard said. Then he looked past us in the direction of the courtyard. "Ah, here she is now."

We both turned in the direction of the courtyard and saw a conservatively dressed woman walking towards us, her long, dark skirt covering her feet as she seemingly glided over the cobbles. Her gray hair was pinned to the top of her head, her face free of any trace of makeup. She was smiling in a guarded way, as if she knew a storm was coming and had to be joyful about it.

"I'm sorry, I wasn't aware there were any guided tours scheduled for today," she said, stopping a few paces away from where we stood outside the glass enclosure.

"I'm afraid there might have been a mix-up," Uri said. The middle-aged woman turned to me, as if for further explanation, but I only smiled, unsure of how to handle this latest hiccup.

"Adira, this gentleman claims to know you," the guard said, leaving the glass enclosure and standing next to Uri.

I saw the color leave Uri's face and his mouth twitch slightly.

"Professor....Nevon, is it?" the guard said.

Uri nodded.

"Nevon..." the older woman said. "Do I know you? I recognize the name but I'm sorry to say I don't recall having ever met before."

Uri looked the woman in the eye steadfastly.

"You sure about that, Adira?" the guard asked.

"Wait..." she said. Her eyes were just as steadfast, narrow and unblinking. "I know who you are. You're...*him*..." She pointed an accusing finger. "The Talpiot tomb troublemaker. And I know why you're here..."

Uri took a step forward. "Wait, I can explain..."

Adira glided backwards a few steps as if announcing her departure. "You're not welcome here. Both of you must leave." And with that she was gone.

"Just as I thought," the guard said. "Police!" His voice echoed through the courtyard.

"Wait!" I called out to the guard and to Adira. "Let us explain!"

"Police!" the guard yelled again just as three uniformed officers ran through the entrance and surrounded Uri and me.

"You'll have plenty of time to explain once you're taken into custody," a booming voice said.

I turned in the direction of the voice and saw Benjamin Schwarz waltzing through the entrance of the complex in our direction. He hadn't changed much in the two years since I'd last seen him. He was a little more gray on top and it looked like he had gained a couple of pounds around the middle. But some things never changed: the all-black wardrobe and black sunglasses.

"Lev told me you'd come back," he said, looking in my direction. "What is it this time? You've found Jesus' body?"

The three uniformed officers chuckled.

"Benjamin, please. Take it easy on her," Uri said.

"Uri, I'm disappointed," Benjamin said. "I thought you'd given up these silly cat-and-mouse games. I thought you were on the straight and narrow now, wanting to put your best foot forward for that new assignment of yours."

My head snapped towards Uri. "What does he mean, Uri?" I asked.

"Later," Uri whispered through the side of his mouth.

"Now, would one of you like to tell me what's going on?" Benjamin asked.

I looked at Uri, who had his eyes trained on Benjamin. "The remains of Saint Peter's ossuary," he said. "We know they're here, hidden somewhere within the complex."

Benjamin didn't need to shield his eyes with sunglasses for me to tell that Uri's words had rattled him. His shoulders tensed and his jaw twitched as he stood silent.

"This...ossuary," he finally said, clearing his throat. "What importance is it to you?"

"That's none of your business!" I hissed. "We just want to see it!"

"Impossible!" the guard suddenly yelled, his voice booming through the courtyard. Benjamin's henchmen instinctively jerked their hands towards their holstered guns. Benjamin put out his hand palm up, as if willing his men to stand down.

"Sir," Benjamin said, walking towards the guard. "Explain the meaning of your sudden outburst."

"There is no such thing as an ossuary belonging to Saint Peter," he said.

"Fine," I said, suddenly impatient with what seemed like intentional dilly-dallying. "The museum has in its possession some ossuary shards with the name Simon bar Jonah etched on them. Does that ring a bell?"

"Yes," the guard said.

"Well, that's what we want to see," I said.

Benjamin turned to Uri. "You claimed earlier that the shards are hidden?"

Uri nodded.

"And you thought you could just march in here and demand to see them?"

"Not exactly," I answered for Uri. Then, sarcastically, "I thought if we asked nicely..."

Ben glided towards me, removing his sunglasses and hooking them through the top of his shirt. He narrowed his eyes at me as if to say, "Who the hell do you think you are?"

Suddenly Benjamin's cell phone rang. He pulled it from his pocket and looked at the display. "None of you move an inch," he said, backing away from the circle to take the call. As he turned his back to us, his three men stepped back and apart from each other in order to better watch us.

Uri took this opportunity to speak to the guard.

"Why are the ossuary shards hidden?"

"They are not hidden," the guard said.

I wanted to hear what the guard had to say, but I had the sense that something was off with Benjamin. What phone call would be important enough for him to excuse himself in the middle of an interrogation? I would have to hear the rest of Uri's conversation with the guard later; at the moment I had the sense that listening in on Benjamin's conversation was more important.

I turned my head, my right ear now trained in Benjamin's direction. I heard him whispering but couldn't make out what he was saying. Out of the corner of my eye I could see the three policemen watching us. I took a few steps back and faked a grimace. One officer sensed my movement and asked if everything was alright.

"Rock in my shoe," I said, untying my shoe. I removed my shoe and balanced on one foot to remove the imaginary rock. Doing so allowed me to fake losing my balance so that I'd have to take a few more steps back. The officer was distracted with watching me remove my shoe that he was unaware of the distance I had created between myself and the rest of the circle. With those few extra steps Benjamin's words came into focus.

"Yes, sir, I have the situation under control." He ran his free hand through his hair and paced back and forth.

"They insist on seeing it. They say it belongs to Saint Peter."

Silence.

"Yes, I know we must not allow them to think that, Sir."

Silence.

"I know that would compromise the plan."

Silence.

"I understand. What would you have me do?"

For once Benjamin seemed to be taking orders, rather than giving them.

"Are you sure?"

Silence.

Benjamin sighed. "Yes, Sir. As you wish."

I quickly put my shoe back on and tied it just as Benjamin was snapping his phone shut. I shuffled forward to rejoin the circle.

"But I must insist that the shards aren't hidden!" the guard was saying. He seemed agitated, tired of answering the same question over and over.

As usual, Uri was calm. "Then they *are* here."

"Yes, of course," the guard said, sounding exasperated. "They've been here for years. In the archives. The remains can't be put on display because they are too fragile."

"But we can still see them if we had permission."

"Of course you can see them," Benjamin said, sliding up behind us. He pulled a handkerchief from his pocket and mopped his forehead.

"But I'm afraid it's too late," the guard said.

"Too late?" I asked. "Why?"

"The ossuary fragments were packed away this morning. They are slated for...relocation."

Uri and I were struck mute by this latest blow.

"Such a shame," Benjamin said. Then he began tapping his chin with a finger as if deep in thought. Finally, he turned to Uri, a serious glint in his eyes. "Let's come to an agreement, shall we?"

"An agreement," Uri said.

"I will make arrangements for you and Miss Beltane to see the ossuary fragments..."

"Today, I hope," I said.

"Yes, right now," Benjamin said.

"*What*?" the guard said. "But—"

Benjamin held up a palm and glared at the guard to silence him.

"You will have full access to the ossuary fragments," Benjamin continued.

"What's the catch?" I asked.

"You must not tell anyone what you saw here today," he said. "If you do, if you tell *anyone* that you saw the ossuary fragments....I can't be held responsible for what might happen to you."

"What the hell does that mean?" I said.

"Fine," Uri interjected, glancing at me and then back to Benjamin. "We won't say a word. To anyone."

"Then it's agreed," Benjamin said. He waved a hand in the air, motioning to the guard. "Let them pass."

And with that, we were in.

CHAPTER NINE

I was underground, that much I knew. I struggled to make my way through complete darkness, stumbling over hard rock and mounds of compacted dirt beneath my feet. A damp, pungent mustiness bombarded my nose. The scratchy material of the blindfold irritated my eyes.

"No one told us this was part of the deal!" I called out. My voice echoed out in front of me into oblivion.

"Slight change in the details," a voice said in my ear. I recognized it as the guard's. He walked slightly behind me to the right, his left hand on my shoulder, guiding and gently pushing me forward. "You *do* want to see the ossuary, right?"

Uri, also blindfolded, was behind the guard. He was being led by one of Ben's men, who remained silent, apparently allowing his Jericho 941 pistol sidearm I'd seen while we were outside to do the talking for him.

Uri and I were being led single-file down a long, narrow passage, only one passage among many in an underground maze of subterranean tunnels.

"Mara yakiri," Uri said. *My dear Mara.* "Save your breath."

"Silence, both of you!" the guard said.

Soon enough we came to a stop and the blindfold was ripped away from my eyes. I blinked and waited for my eyes to come into focus on our new surroundings. Instinctively I searched for Uri, who was a few steps to my right, also attempting to adjust his eyes to the new level of light.

We were in a small chamber, perhaps 20 foot square. Small lanterns mounted around the perimeter walls cast an eerie glow and menacing shadows on the floor. In the center of the room was a large slab table, illuminated by an overhead spotlight. A cloth was spread out on the table, and on it, several small fragments of stone and one large slab of stone.

"Are you all right?" Uri said.

"I'm fine," I said. Then, turning to the guard I said, "Although I think the blindfolds were a bit much."

The guard shrugged, as if the blindfolds were not his idea. "You heard what Chief Schwarz said. You mustn't tell anyone what you saw here today. The blindfolds are to ensure you don't see too much."

"Fine, whatever," I said, turning away from the guard. "Are you okay, Uri?"

He nodded and turned his attention to the contents on the table.

"Some final ground rules," the guard said, stepping between Uri and the table. "You have been given twenty minutes with the ossuary fragments. You are allowed to look, but not to touch. I will be out in the hallway, while my friend here will remain in the room, watching your every move. So no funny stuff..."

As if on cue, the policeman glared at each of us and motioned to his holstered pistol. The guard left through a large, heavy door I don't remember entering, slamming it shut behind him.

Our twenty minutes had begun.

The policeman stepped back into the shadows as Uri scanned the contents of the table.

"Look at that large piece," I said, walking around the table to get a better look at it. Clearly it was a corner piece of a rectangular ossuary. On the longer side was an inscription. "What's it say?"

Uri came around the other side of the table to join me, leaning closer to the table to read the inscription. His eyes scanned the inscription several times.

"Simon bar Jonah," he finally said. "The inscription reads Simon bar Jonah."

"Simon son of Jonah?" I said, translating into English. "Are you telling me this is it?"

Uri nodded. "You may be looking at the vessel that held the sacred remains of Saint Peter."

At that moment it felt as if a gentle shock of electricity coursed through my body, making my skin tingle, my hair stand on end, my eyes flood with tears.

Instinctively I reached out to touch the stone box. From the shadows the policeman cleared his throat, reminding me that we were still being watched. But I didn't care. I needed release from the excitement coursing through me. I reached for Uri's hand instead.

"This...this is incredible," I said, motioning to the shards on the table with my free hand. "These might prove that Saint Peter wasn't martyred in Rome."

Uri squeezed my hand and looked at me tenderly, smiling. We stood silent for a moment, lost in our own private thoughts. But then his face changed. His smile faded, and the look in his eyes betrayed something different.

Disappointment.

Uri slowly released my hand.

"What is it?" I asked. "What's wrong?"

He sighed and caressed my shoulder and a bolt of lightning when through me. He glanced over at the guard, still shrouded in the shadows.

"What's going on?" I said.

"Peter spent time in Rome...and was killed there."

"How...how can you possibly know that?" I said. "Peter undoubtedly led the first Jerusalem church. He is among the first witnesses of the resurrection. He dedicated so much of his life preaching to his brethren in and around Judea. So why would he leave and go to Rome?"

"Keep in mind that although some of the apostles chose to stay near the churches they founded, it was their universal mission to preach the message of Jesus to all nations, Jews and Gentiles alike. Peter, as

Prince of the Apostles, certainly would have traveled extensively. We know, for example, that he was the first bishop of Antioch for several years, before moving on to other areas east of Judea, before meeting his fate in Rome. And everywhere he went—"

"Wait," I interrupted. "So Peter met his fate in Rome?"

"Yes."

"But isn't the point of our mission to prove that Peter never *set foot* in Rome?"

"Mara, there is no doubt that Peter traveled to Rome. The Roman Empire ruled half of the known world at the time. Naturally he'd want to reach all the populations living under the superstitious and hedonistic Romans."

"But what about what you said yesterday at Dominus Flevit? About how neither the New Testament nor Peter himself indicated that he'd ever traveled to Rome..."

"I remember what I said."

"You seemed convinced that had Peter gone to Rome, someone somewhere, somehow would've made note of it. After all, that's pretty important information...you said so yourself."

"It would be akin to leaving the Acts of the Apostles out of the Bible..."

"Right. So now you're saying Peter *did* go to Rome?"

"Yesterday I was presenting only one side of the argument," Uri said. "You know me. I prefer to present the evidence I know, and allow you to draw your own conclusions."

"My conclusion is that we're getting nowhere fast..."

Uri took my hand. "My dear Mara, Peter occupied Rome and was crucified there."

"Is that your personal opinion, or well-attested facts?"

"There may not be archeological or written evidence of his—"

"Then what's the point of all this?" I interrupted, ripping my hand from his grasp. "Why lead me on this wild goose chase?"

Uri closed his eyes and sighed. "Mara, you're trying to answer the wrong questions."

"What do you mean?" I said, my raised voice echoing through the small chamber. "The questions I'm trying to answer are pretty cut and dry. Did Peter go to Rome or not? Was he crucified in Rome or not...?"

Do you care for me, Uri Nevon, or not?

That thought came out of nowhere, no doubt brought on in light of the hand-holding and shoulder caressing and intense eye contact that had been happening between us since we'd first been reunited in Saint Peter's Square. But I had to let the thought go, because that situation was also going nowhere fast. And now was neither the time nor the place.

"The question is not, Did Peter travel to Rome?" Uri said, bringing me back to the subject at hand. "Because he most certainly did. The question should be, Did he travel there only intermittently, or was he seated there for twenty-five years as the city's first Pope, as tradition dictates? Similarly, the question is not, Did Peter die in Rome—because he most certainly did—but was Peter *buried* in Rome? Do you see the difference?"

I sighed, knowing yet again Uri was right and I had failed to prove a point. "Fine. So I've been asking the wrong questions."

"A name on a bone box is not enough conclusive evidence to prove that it belonged to Saint Peter. As rare a find as it is..."

"Great. So now what?"

"We must discover the rest of Peter's story."

"How do we do that?"

"Return to Rome."

"But we just got to Jerusalem."

"This is the next step in our journey, Mara. This is how it must be." Then he took a step forward, so close I could feel his breath on my face. "But before we go, there is one more thing you must keep in mind."

"And that is?"

"The New Testament doesn't mention a lot of things about Saint Peter. But perhaps those are just omissions."

"Omissions?"

"An omission is simply that—an omission. It isn't an indicator of truth. So, just because the New Testament doesn't say Peter traveled to Rome, doesn't mean that he didn't."

Just then there was a noise at the door. A jangling of keys.

I continued Uri's line of thinking. "Which could also mean that just because there's no archeological or historical proof indicating that Peter was buried in Jerusalem, doesn't mean that he wasn't..."

More noise at the door. The click of a lock disengaging. The loud thud of a heavy door being pushed open. Twenty minutes couldn't possibly have passed already.

Uri kept talking, as if unaware that our time was up. He was still close, and he whispered, "...And just because I don't tell you that I love you doesn't mean that I don't..."

"Time's up!" the guard bellowed, barging through the door.

I froze in place, unable to do anything except search Uri's face.

"Wh...what?" I finally managed.

He touched a piece of my hair, continuing to speak softly. "Sometimes it's the things that aren't said that will lead you to the truth you seek. You just need to search a little harder, dig a little deeper."

I didn't have time to respond. The policeman emerged from the shadows and the guard rushed towards us. I caught a last glimpse of Uri's brown eyes just as the policeman grabbed me, a blindfold plunging me into darkness.

PART TWO
CHAPTER TEN

• • • •

WE WERE NOT WELCOMED back to Rome.

While we was in Jerusalem, forces—powerful, influential forces—were anticipating our return.

Gathering their army.

Planning their attack.

They wanted to silence me and Uri, and they'd soon prove they'd go to extreme measures to do so.

They knew we were close to the truth, and they couldn't afford this truth to see the light of day.

At least that's how I justified what they did to me.

What they did to Uri.

And the truth was this: That although Saint Peter may have travelled to Rome, preached to the heathens across the Roman Empire, he was not buried there. His remains were not underneath the cavernous cathedral that bears his name. After all, he was until his dying day a son of Jerusalem, a Jew by birth, and would return to Jerusalem in a stone box that declared, "Simon, son of Jonah." And there, in the city of his birth, Simon son of Jonah would rest for all eternity.

At least that's what I believed was the secret they were trying to protect.

Were it true, it meant the Catholic Church had been lying to two billion followers of their own faith—indeed, the whole world—for nearly two thousand years.

That hidden truth could have unimaginable consequences.

It could incite riots.

A frenzied media.

Millions of defections from Catholicism.

Millions in lost papal revenue.

Perhaps even all-out warfare.

And the truth could get me and Uri killed.

The truth had the power to change the entire world as we know it.

And so help me God, I was determined to uncover the truth.

There was a heavy price to pay, of course.

And I would surely suffer the consequences.

CHAPTER ELEVEN

A t the time of Jesus' death, in the third decade of the first century, the Roman Empire ruled half of the known world. Its territory and influence stretched across northern Europe, south into Africa, and east into the Middle East and Asia.

Because of the empire's vast extent and thousand-year endurance, Rome had a profound influence on everything from language and law, to art and culture, to religion and philosophy.

Tiberius was emperor during Jesus' time spent in Roman-ruled Jerusalem, but his name is mentioned only once or twice in the bible. His legacy is that of a great Roman general, but an aloof, dark, and reclusive emperor.

And he was known for his disdain for the Jews.

During his reign, Tiberius banished Jewish people from Rome, threatening to enslave them if they refused to leave the city.

Less than two decades later, at the time of Jesus' death, there was a new emperor seated in Rome, the one Saint Peter would come to know well.

Nero.

During Nero's reign, the Christians were increasing in number and influence across the Roman Empire. Nero, having little use for the Christian leaders and followers, started a campaign to wipe them out. Peter was a prime target, as he was a leader of the Christian community and well known in Rome at the time. Under orders from Emperor Nero, Peter was to be crucified.

Upon his request, Peter was crucified upside down, because he claimed he was not worthy enough to be crucified in the same manner as Jesus Christ.

Tradition dictates that his body was buried in Rome, in the crypt under the basilica that bears his name.

I was back in Rome to prove otherwise.

My first stop: the basilica of Saint John Lateran.

"Tell me why we're here again," I asked Uri, craning my neck to take in the height of its columned façade.

"It is the mother church of Roman Catholics," Uri explained. "The oldest of the four papal basilicas, and the seat of the Bishop of Rome."

"The oldest basilica in Rome? Even older than Saint Peter's?"

"It is older than and ranks above Saint Peter's."

I was surprised by this revelation, that given the pomp and circumstance surrounding Saint Peter's basilica, another basilica ranked higher in importance. That's something they don't tell you in the history books.

"A little-known secret among Christians?" I asked, and Uri smiled. "Perhaps."

"There seems to be a lot of secret keeping going on around here," I whispered, returning my attention to the Baroque majesty of the building towering in front of us.

I hadn't intended to say the words out loud. They just came to me in a fit of frustration.

Uri had chosen the most inopportune time to reveal his feelings for me. It was a secret that came most unexpectedly at a time when I was powerless to react or respond.

Professor Uri Nevon was in love with me.

Or so I thought.

I couldn't know for sure because he didn't broach the subject again. He didn't clarify his words, explain his actions, describe his feelings.

Of course, I hadn't helped matters any. I chose to ignore what he said, out of fear that I hadn't heard him correctly, that it was all a dream, that I'd wake in a panic in my condo in Philadelphia and realize that Uri Nevon was just a construct in my mind, a Prince Charming my subconscious had created to fill an emotional void. So I said nothing, not during the long march out the catacombs minutes later, not during our flight back to Rome the previous evening, not during the breakfast we shared that morning.

So for now Uri's words hung out there, alone, unexplained, unrequited.

Uri cleared his throat. "Shall we go inside? There's something I want you to see."

Once inside we made our way down the arched nave, as giant, robed marble apostles reached out to us from their recessed niches. The floor was a mosaic of swirls and circles and serpentine lines. It was not unlike other Byzantine churches I'd found myself in and yet, somehow completely different and new.

We stood for a moment in the nave, and Uri spun around in every direction as if looking for someone, his face a stone mask. Finally, a smile. He found who he'd been looking for.

Dr. Giovanni Maderno.

The professor approached us, waving emphatically and speaking in broken English.

"Uri, my amico, so nice to see you again!" The two men shook hands and embraced. Then he turned to me. "Ciao, Miss Beltane!" He kissed my cheek.

"Hello, Professor Maderno," I said.

"Per favore, call me Giovanni."

"Yes, of course," I said.

Suddenly his face changed from excitement to confusion to concern as he looked at each of us in turn. "So...I am to give you a tour of the basilica of Saint John Lateran."

"Is that so?" I said, smiling and turning to Uri. "Will Professor Nevon be joining us?"

"Mara, I—" Uri started, looking at me with pleading eyes. He cleared his throat and continued. "There is something very important I must do. I will call you later." Then he turned to Giovanni. "Grazie,

Giovanni. I remain forever in your debt." The men shook hands and Uri retreated back down the nave without glancing back.

The first time I was left in Giovanni's care I was distracted by notions of Uri's uncertain feelings for me. Did he miss me when I went back to the States? Had he thought of our time together in Jerusalem? This time, only a few days later, I think I knew the answers. Yet it didn't bring me any closer to comfort.

"Such tension!" Giovanni was saying as my thoughts reverted back to the matter at hand. "I had no idea…"

"What do you mean?"

"I had no idea you had such a hold on Uri."

"That's ridiculous!" I said, perhaps too loudly. An older couple turned to look at us as if to shush us into silence. I lowered my voice and took a step closer to the professor. "What are you talking about?"

"I haven't seen Uri act like that since…well now, let me think…" Giovanni started counting in Italian, staring at the richly decorated gold-leaf ceiling. It was obvious he was talking to himself now. "I've really only seen him act so disheveled once before in the presence of a woman and that was with Ziva, which means…" He jerked his face down from the ceiling and gawked at me wide-eyed. "What happened in Jerusalem?"

"Nothing," I said, thrown by the mention of Ziva. "Nothing happened in Jerusalem."

How did he even know we'd gone to Jerusalem?

"Ah ha!" Giovanni said, pointing an index finger in the air. "Nothing happened in Jerusalem and yet everything became clear. Am I right?"

Was this guy psychic? "Something like that."

"You Americans! So modest! If I was in amore or had the love of a beautiful woman I would be screaming it from the rooftops!" Giovanni threw his hands up in the air.

"Why do you keep insisting Uri and I are in love?"

The professor shook his head at me. "What did I tell you the first time we met about a person's eyes?"

I thought a moment. "The eyes tell all?"

"Exactly! Gli occhi dicono tutto. I've known Uri for nearly twenty years. He is a reserved man, not one to display his emotions easily..."

"You can say that again," I whispered.

"...Yet his eyes betray him," he continued as if he hadn't heard me. "Signora, Uri Nevon is most certainly in love with you. And if I had to guess, judging by the look in your eyes when Uri rushed out of here, I would say the feeling is mutual."

"I...I don't know how to respond to that."

"No need," Giovanni said, motioning me forward farther down the nave. "I know why you are here."

"I'm glad someone does."

Giovanni seemed to ignore my comment. With a few more steps we found ourselves beneath a triumphal arch in the middle of the transept, staring at the Gothic papal altar.

"This magnificent building has been burned and sacked and ravaged and rebuilt many times," Giovanni said. "But I'm not going to bore you with history when the most important thing you need to know is before you."

"The wooden altar?" I ventured a guess.

"Saint Peter himself is said to have celebrated Mass at this altar. But no, there is something more important here."

My mind was swimming with so many thoughts that I couldn't even begin to guess what Giovanni was trying to say. I could only shrug.

Giovanni continued. "Most people believe that the remains of Saint Peter are buried beneath Saint Peter's basilica." He paused, took a breath and continued. "But most do not realize that a relic of Saint Peter also lies here, hidden in this altar."

"By relic do you mean...a body part?"

The professor closed his eyes and nodded.

"His heart."

CHAPTER TWELVE

G*ive him time.*
He needs to process his feelings.
He'll reveal his intentions when the time is right...

Giovanni's words bounced around in my brain as I made my way up Capitoline Hill, one of the Seven Hills of Rome, and the geographical and ceremonial center of ancient Rome. Few ancient buildings actually remain; they'd been covered up over the ensuing centuries by Medieval and Renaissance palaces surrounding Michelangelo's Piazza del Campidoglio.

My final destination was the northeastern slope of the hill, at the 17th century San Giuseppe dei Falegnami Catholic Church. In the bowels of the church an ancient site remains, a place so venerated by Catholics it was turned into a shrine, complete with an altar emblazoned with an upside-down cross.

Mamertine Prison.

It is here where Saint Peter was said to be imprisoned under orders of Emperor Nero. It is here that Saint Peter baptized his guards using a spring he miraculously created. And it is here that an angel descended from heaven in the middle of the night and freed him and his cell mate, Saint Paul.

Or so the story goes.

I would find out more when I met with Uri. No doubt he'd present some interesting topics to ponder, perhaps about faith, historical truth, or the possibility of miracles.

Now if I could only clear my mind of Giovanni's advice about cutting Uri some slack....

His emotions scare him. Have faith in the fact that he loves you. Be patient and you will be rewarded. You will have your happy ending.

So says the professor and part-time prophet.

The sun was high when I found Uri standing outside the raised façade of the San Giuseppe dei Falegnami. My stomach lurched at the thought of yet another meeting where Uri and I tip-toed around the truth.

It was another beautiful spring day. Children danced across the cobbled square. Locals lounged on the grass, their faces raised to the sun, gelatos in hand. Tourists scurried by, their noses buried in guide books.

Uri, on the other hand, was a study in guardedness. There was no jollity on his face, and he stood off to the side where the sun had cast a shadow. His hands were stuffed into his blazer pockets and his shoulders were tensed as if shaken with cold. And perhaps most curiously, he occasionally jerked his head over his shoulder as if at any moment someone would sneak up behind him.

As I approached I noticed his usually twinkling eyes were missing that spark of joy that usually marked the start of a new day's adventure. He looked pale and tired.

Something was very wrong, and I doubted he would tell me what.

"Mara," he said, more out of relief than a greeting. Then he smiled weakly. "Did you find your way here okay?"

I nodded, studying his face. "Everything okay?"

"Yes, of course." He cleared his throat. "Are you ready?"

Before I had a chance to respond, Uri grabbed my hand and led me down a flight of stairs through a trapezoidal upper prison room, and then down a second flight of steps into the lower room of the prison, where Saint Peter was supposedly kept.

He ushered me inside the small, circular room, looking over my shoulder as I crossed the threshold. We were in the deepest part of the complex, a secret room where condemned prisoners were detained before execution.

We were alone in the room. Uri took a minute to catch his breath, and I looked around the room for the tell-tale signs of Saint Peter's presence: etchings on the wall where he marked out his days; the stone column that Saints Peter and Paul were chained to; the spring that Peter miraculously created to baptize his captors.

"We mustn't spend much time here," Uri finally said, still catching his breath.

"Why? We've got plenty—"

"There's still so much to see!" Uri interrupted, somewhat impatiently, glancing over my shoulder again at the entrance to the room.

"Okay, okay," I said, attempting to calm the anxiety that was overtaking him.

"Mara, I'm sorry," Uri said, reaching out to take my hand. I rebuffed him, crossing my arms in front of me and turning away, lest he see the tears welling up in my eyes.

This seemed an appropriate place for us to be at the moment. Uri's emotions seemed to be imprisoned inside him, unable to be revealed, and I felt much like a locked up prisoner would—lost, desperate, hopeless.

"Just tell me what you want me to know and then we'll go, okay?"

Uri stepped forward and caressed my hair. "I just want you to know that..." Then he took a step back, searched the ceiling, and sighed. "That perhaps miracles aren't possible. That as much as we want them to be, angels aren't real. That when our faith is tested, even the strongest among us falter."

There was a long pause and I searched Uri's eyes for hidden meaning. He could have been talking about Saint Peter. That since miracles aren't possible, there's no way he could've made a spring appear out of thin air in which to baptize his prison guards. That since angels don't exist, there's no way an ethereal being came down from heaven and freed him from this prison. And that since there's no reliable evidence that Saint Peter was imprisoned here, we can't rely on faith alone for the answers.

But perhaps he was speaking about himself. That with such insurmountable odds facing us, it would take a miracle to solve the riddle of Saint Peter's burial. That it would take our own logic and reasoning—and not divine intervention—to lead us on the right path. And that, with scant evidence to prove Saint Peter was buried in Jerusalem, Uri's faith in that belief—indeed, in *himself*—was faltering.

At that moment it didn't really matter who Uri was talking about. I could see pain in his eyes. He was suffering, most likely because of me. Uri was putting himself on the line for me, again. So even if he couldn't profess his feelings yet, I could. It was time for me to step up and let him know how I felt.

"I respectfully disagree," I said. "I believe it was a miracle that allowed us to meet. That an angel is watching over us, keeping us together. And I want you to know that my faith in you has never, ever faltered."

Uri smiled but remained silent.

I took a deep breath and decided to take a risk. "I love you."

Uri took both my hands in his. "Thank you, Mara, for everything you said. But I don't...I mean, we can't—"

"Don't do this," I interrupted, backing away from him. Tears started to blur my vision. I couldn't tell at first if they were tears borne out of sadness or anger. Perhaps both.

He took a step closer. "Don't do what?"

"Pretend you don't care. About me. About us..."

"What do you want me to say?" There was frustration in his voice.

"Whatever's in here!" I said, pushing into his chest with an index finger.

Uri sighed heavily. "Please understand..."

"Just say something, anything!"

There was a moment of silence as my angry voice disappeared into the thin air of the small chamber. My breaths were short and quick and I scarcely think I heard Uri breathing at all. Suddenly his eyes locked with mine and I saw something different written on his face. Resoluteness? Clarity?

"When we were underground at the Church of the Flagellation I told you I loved you," he said. "That was a mistake."

"What?" I said, sobbing.

"I shouldn't have said it."

At that moment it felt like the aftermath of a bomb blast. Uri's lips were moving, and he was gesturing at me, but all sound was blocked by the intense ringing that had suddenly arisen in my ears. After a few seconds I caught muffled words and phrases underneath the ringing.

"...*Mara, I can't...*"

"...*not now...*"

"...*too little time...*"

"...*more complicated than you think...*"

I pressed my hands to my ears in a vain attempt to dull the ringing sound.

"I have to go," I heard myself say.

I saw Uri's lips mouth the word, "What?"

I repeated myself.

"Don't go," he said.

But it was too late. I turned and ran up the steps, tripping when I neared the top. I grabbed the handrail to pull myself up and caught a glimpse of a plaque on the wall naming some of the prisoners who'd met their fates here. I scanned the list of names and expected to see my own. It felt like I was about to be executed.

From down below I heard Uri's voice echo up the stairs. "Mara, wait!"

Without hesitation, I lunged for the next set of stairs that would take me aboveground to the bright light of day. What the onlookers and passersby must have thought, seeing me running down the street, sobbing, mumbling incoherently.

All I know is that I didn't stop running until I had reached my hotel room, where I crashed on the bed in a fit of anger and hysterics and eventually cried myself to sleep.

CHAPTER THIRTEEN

I woke to the sound of the phone ringing. I was in my hotel room, on top of the covers, fully dressed.

I glanced at the alarm clock on the bedside table.

3:09 p.m.

I'd slept for two hours, but it felt like two days. Without even looking in a mirror I could tell my eyes were puffy and swollen.

I answered the phone.

"Good afternoon, Miss Beltane," a male accented voice said. "There's a note at the front desk for you. You can retrieve it at your convenience."

"A note? From who?"

"I don't know, Miss. He didn't leave his name."

Uri.

Who else?

I thought for a moment before responding.

"I'll be down in a few minutes."

I sat on the edge of the bed, thinking. A long walk would help clear my head, I finally decided. Most of the sites would be starting to close for the day, but at the very least I could get something to eat and soak in more of the city. All I really wanted to do anyway was get lost for a little while.

On my way through the lobby I retrieved the note and put it in my pocket. I would read it later, once I'd purged my mind of the anger and frustration I still had for Uri.

I made my way to the closest subway stop and decided to take it to Termini Station, where I'd explore further the area Uri and I had had dinner my first night in town. From Termini Station I could get just about anywhere in the city, should the urge arise to go somewhere else.

During the brief subway ride I reviewed my map and guide book and realized that Sapienza University is within walking distance of

Termini Station. That was it, then. I would grab a bite to eat, read the mysterious note, and then on a whim pay a visit to Professor Maderno.

• • • •

MARA,

I had to return to Jerusalem to take care of an urgent business matter. My apologies for leaving so hastily. I will return in two days' time and we'll pick up where we left off.

Uri

I put the note in my back pocket and took another bite of *pizza à taglio*, a slice of pizza rolled up in wax paper for easy on-the-go eating.

Wasn't it just like Uri to leave out important details, I thought, wiping sauce from my mouth. An audience of pigeons circled my feet, and another boldly sat on the bench next to me, hoping for a handout. I tossed the last pieces of crust on the sidewalk and the birds wasted no time in pecking away until even the smallest of crumbs had been consumed.

Gathering my things and making my way to the main campus of Sapienza University, I convinced myself Uri would explain himself in good time.

But maybe he wouldn't.

First he hinted that he loved me, then he took it back. He said it was "a mistake." Did he mean loving me was a mistake? Or that telling me he loved me was a mistake?

Either way, I couldn't let the current state of our relationship interfere with my mission. Admittedly, things weren't going to plan in Rome. Sure, professionally-speaking Uri and I were making headway, visiting the important sites in Peter's life, learning about his martyrdom and crucifixion. It felt like we were getting closer to the truth.

But on a personal level, we were a disaster. Things would work out the way they were supposed to, but until then, I just hoped it wouldn't derail our mission.

What had I been thinking? Uri and I hadn't seen in each other in nearly two years. Did I think we could simply pick up where we left off, as if no time had elapsed? Had I daydreamed Ziva out of existence and erased all Uri's memories of her? Did I dupe myself into believing that two people of disparate cultures, religions and backgrounds could fall in love simply and seamlessly? Had I duped myself into believing that Uri could love me at all...?

This is exactly what Jenny had warned me about. Turns out she knew me better than I knew myself. I had fallen into the trap, just like she said I would. Because of unrealistic expectations, Rome had disappointed me a second time.

Funny how preconceived notions of a city turn out to be more romantic than the truth.

I followed the signs to the building that housed the architectural sciences department. Giovanni's voice echoed in my head.

Patience.

Uri will reveal himself when the time is right.

I found his office on the first floor and, peeking my head inside, found that he was just wrapping up with a student. When he saw me, he ushered me inside with a kiss to the cheek and bade me sit down.

"To what do I owe the pleasure?" he asked, sitting down behind his desk.

"I was in the neighborhood," I said, suddenly realizing that there really was no particular reason for my visit. Perhaps I just needed a fatherly voice of reason to calm my anxiety.

"Where is Uri?"

"Jerusalem."

"What could be so important there that he is not here with you?"

"An urgent business matter, apparently."

Giovanni studied my face, his gray eyebrows furrowed. "Do I sense trouble in paradise?"

"No offense, professor, but can we not talk about Uri?"

"Of course, signora. No Uri talk. So tell me—how can I help you?"

"Well," I said, deciding that I probably should have a valid reason for disturbing him. "I thought maybe you had a few minutes to tell me about your ancestor, Carlo?"

"Ah, dear Carlo," Giovanni said, a far-off look in his eyes. "He was born in 1556 in an Italian-speaking section of southern Switzerland. He got his start in the marble quarries of northern Switzerland before moving to Rome in 1588..."

It was then that I remembered Giovanni's teaching style: just the facts, all of them, laid out end to end ad nauseam until you thought your brain would explode from the sheer volume of information. I would have to ask him pointed questions if I wished to get to the heart of what I wanted to know.

"And his experience with marble....it led to him becoming an architect?"

"Most certainly. And his uncle played a role in that. Carlo worked as a marble cutter for his uncle in Rome, through whom he learned the craft of sculpting marble."

"That workmanship helped Carlo earn the title of one of the fathers of Italian Baroque architecture. Is that right?"

The professor leaned forward in his chair and grinned. "Someone's been doing her homework."

I smiled and shrugged.

"So the comment you made when we first met about Carlo being pressured to change Michelangelo's design of Saint Peter's Basilica...?"

"Yes! By the time Carlo was hired as lead architect of Saint Peter's, Michelangelo had been dead for forty years. His original design didn't encompass all the hallowed ground on which the current building stood. Carlo was hesitant to deviate from Michelangelo's set design, but the Pope said no way! The nave must be lengthened to make the interior of the building larger. Carlo had no choice but to obey."

"And the façade Carlo re-designed?"

"Thrown together quickly and hastily built...one of the least liked parts of the whole basilica..."

"What? The façade is the first thing people see!"

The professor laughed. "Those are critics speaking. But they have a point: the breadth of the façade—not to mention the length of the nave—blocks the view of the dome from the piazza out front! The only way to see the whole dome is from a distance or from up on high..."

I closed my eyes and pictured myself standing in Saint Peter's square looking up at the façade and the dome beyond it. In my mind's eye I saw only the top half of the dome, small and demure against the sweeping height of the façade. Giovanni was right. It was as if Michaelangelo's famous dome was more of an afterthought than an integral part of the design. A small cherry plopped on top of a heaping pile of whipped cream, lost and drowning and screaming for attention.

"Can you see it?" Giovanni asked and I opened my eyes.

I nodded.

"From the front, the basilica has no vertical feature to it," he continued. "It looks flat!"

"So why was it built that way?"

"Several Popes had overseen the building of the basilica over many decades. Pope Paul V, who hired Carlo, wanted papal blessings to be conducted from the balcony above the central door. And he wanted it to appear palatial. So he made Carlo extend the façade."

"It certainly looks palatial," I said. "So as an architect what do you think of your ancestor's design?"

"Naturally, I think Carlo was a genius! Criticisms aside, and in spite of papal pressure, he created something truly magnificent, even if Michelangelo still to this day gets most of the credit."

"Did Carlo inspire you to get into architecture?"

"Certainly. Building design runs deep in my family. It has coursed through the Maderno blood for nearly 500 years."

"I appreciate you taking the time to enlighten me," I said. Then, thinking I had taken up enough of his time, I gathered my things to go.

But the professor sat up straight and said, "Now, tell me—how was your little side trip to Jerusalem?"

"You knew about that?"

"Uri informed me you were going but I haven't been in touch with him since your return. So, what were your findings?"

"We saw the supposed ossuary of Saint Peter," I said, and Giovanni's eyes widened. "The inscription on it undisputedly reads 'Simon son of Jonah.'"

"The ossuary remains are housed at the Church of the Flagellation, no?"

"That's right. Perhaps we are one step closer to discovering Peter's true resting place." Then, thinking perhaps Uri hadn't shared our mission with the professor I asked, "You do know that's why I'm in Rome, right?"

"To prove that Peter is buried in Jerusalem and not under the basilica. You said as much the day we met." Giovanni winked at me. "Among other things..."

"Right," I said, suddenly remembering how much I had revealed during our tour of Saint Peter's basilica. Hopefully he would continue to leave the subject of Uri alone.

"How do you feel about our mission?" I asked.

"Well, I assume the goal is to create controversy and sensationalism to sell books." Then he smirked at me. "But I also assume that you won't find the evidence to disprove long-standing tradition."

"You don't think so?"

"I am a religious man by birth, so my heart tells me Peter is in Rome. But I am a man of science by trade, so I must believe in the possibility of his burial in Jerusalem."

"Do you think I'm on a fool's mission?"

"Miss Beltane, I'm not one to dash anyone's dreams."

"Call me Mara," I corrected him.

Giovanni nodded. "Si, signora."

"The ossuary we saw in Jerusalem could be interpreted as pretty convincing evidence."

"It could be the real thing, it could not. I am an architect, not an archeologist. Who am I to say?"

"Fair enough. I appreciate your honesty," I said. "But understand my mission isn't just about selling books. I want to start a dialogue. I want to get people talking about the possibility of Peter's burial in Jerusalem."

"And naturally you want to be on the best-sellers lists again," Giovanni said.

"That would be an added bonus," I admitted.

"Do you think the ossuary you saw in Jerusalem could possibly be the bone box of Peter? Because make no mistake: your novel's mission is to make people believe it to be true. You must convince people that he was buried in Jerusalem."

"Or sell them on the *possibility* that he was buried in Jerusalem," I countered. "And considering everything we had to go through just to see a few ossuary shards, I believe it's possible."

Giovanni narrowed his eyes. "What do you mean?"

"We were begrudgingly taken to see the ossuary. In blindfolds."

At this, Giovanni leaned forward, his chin nearly touching the table.

"What? Did Uri know this in advance?"

"I think so. I mean, he did warn me."

"Warn you of what?"

"That we'd be trying to extract secrets from the..." I struggled to remember the name of the organization Uri mentioned. "The...Ordo Fratrum Minorum."

"The Ordo Fratrum Minorum," Giovanni repeated.

"Who or what are they?"

"Franciscans, my dear. The Order of the Friars Minor, a religious order that adheres to the teachings and disciplines of Saint Francis of Assisi, the movement's Medieval founder. There are different groups of Franciscans, the Ordo Fratrum Minorum being the most prominent."

"I'm not sure I understand. Uri made them out to be highly secretive and all-powerful. But how bad could they be? They're a bunch of friars!"

"They have been members of the Catholic Church for eight hundred years. And their history is quite twisted."

"So what do the Franciscans have to do with the Custody of the Holy Land?"

"The Custody of the Holy Land..."

"Uri called them the 'guardians of Christendom's holy places.'"

"There are Franciscan custodies all over the world. The Custody of the Holy Land is the group of friars who are stationed across biblical lands—Israel, Egypt, Jordan..."

"Uri said that it was the Custody of the Holy Land that was in possession of the Peter ossuary. Why the secrecy in seeing it? The blindfolds? And why were the Jerusalem police involved?"

"The Franciscans are the largest religious community within the Catholic Church," Giovanni said. "I'm sure they had their reasons."

It was my job now to find out those reasons. What was the Catholic Church trying to hide? What were the Franciscans helping them hide? Who was Benjamin talking to on the phone, and why did that person on the other end seem to be controlling him? And why, after hanging up after a heated discussion, did Benjamin suddenly allow us to see Saint Peter's ossuary?

Whatever the reasons, they were the cause of Uri's subsequent skittishness and paranoia.

Giovanni looked me dead in the eye. "Sounds like you need Uri now more than ever."

CHAPTER FOURTEEN

The Via Appia was conceived for war.

As the ancient Roman republic's first super highway, the Via Appia, or Appian Way, was constructed as a military road in the fourth century BC to usher troops and supplies en masse out of Rome. Over the ensuing decades the Via Appia continued to be built, stretching 400 miles southeast through Italy to important port cities for trade purposes.

The Via Appia is one of the earliest Roman roads ever built, and strategically one of the most important. And, some would say, the most *historically* important. For it is on this road, within two miles of Rome's city center, that Saint Peter attempted to escape persecution at the hand of Emperor Nero.

I looked down at the interlocking stones of the 2,500-year-old road and marveled at the thought that Peter might have walked this same path.

Looking up again, at the building in front of me, I was reminded why I was here.

Domine Quo Vadis.

It was on this spot where Peter, newly freed from Mamertine Prison and deciding to flee the city, had a vision of Jesus and asked him where he was going.

"Domine, quo vadis?" Peter asked.

Lord, where are you going?

Jesus replied, "Eo Romam iterum crucifigi."

I am going to Rome to be crucified again.

Apparently Peter's vision of Jesus had such a profound effect on him that he immediately turned around and accepted his fate; he would return to Rome, continue his ministry, and eventually be martyred by Nero.

Today there's a church on the spot where Peter had his vision, the Church of Domine Quo Vadis, a sanctuary built in the 17th century. I stood outside it, more interested in the historical happenings that occurred outside on the road than the modest interior of this small church.

Truth be told, I was here for one other reason.

Unity.

If I was going to understand Peter, I needed to travel where he traveled, walk the same paths, find common ground.

And the common ground that united us, the tie that bound us, was acceptance. Upon seeing the vision of Jesus, Peter realized that he couldn't escape the fate that God intended for him. To show his allegiance to Jesus, to be his one true Apostle, he must return to Rome and accept whatever awaited him there.

Likewise, I must accept that perhaps Uri and I weren't meant to be. And that his feelings towards me, whatever they were, would remain concealed until he was ready to reveal them.

As I pondered, perhaps too long, about my own fate, my cell phone rang. The display read "private."

"Miss Mara?" the voice on the other end said.

"Lev?"

"Miss Mara, thank goodness! Are you all right?"

"Yes, Lev. Of course. Why wouldn't I be?"

"I...I don't know."

"Are you okay?"

"I'm okay," he said, sounding uncertain.

"Listen, have you seen Uri? He said he was returning to Jerusalem for a few days..."

"I, well, yes...he visited me."

"Good. I was starting to worry. He said he was coming back in two days, which is tomorrow, but he's been acting kind of funny lately..."

"Funny?"

"Guarded. Reclusive. Always looking over his shoulder. Did he seem that way to you?"

"Maybe, I don't know..."

"Lev, what's going on? Why did Uri visit you?"

"Mara, I don't have a lot of time. Please don't tell Uri I called you. He'd be upset at me."

"Why? What's happening? You're starting to freak me out."

"You're sure you're okay in Rome by yourself?"

"I'm fine."

There was silence on Lev's end. Finally he whispered, "Just be careful."

"Lev, what did Uri say to you? Why did he go back to Jerusalem?"

"I can't...I can't, Miss Mara. I'm sorry."

On the other end of the phone I heard the tinkle of the door chime and male voices. Two men, maybe more, had entered Lev's store. Lev let out a sudden inhale of breath.

"I have to go!" he said. "Don't tell Uri I called you!"

The male voices grew louder, as if they were approaching Lev. One of the men, with a gruff voice, said something to Lev in Hebrew.

Somehow that voice sounded familiar to me. But I couldn't place it...

"Lev? Are you there? What's happening?"

"Be careful, Miss Mara!" he said. "They might come for you!"

And then the line went dead.

With shaking hands I put my cell phone back inside my bag. I looked around me, at tourists walking the Via Appia, and suddenly felt their eyes on me. One by one they noticed me, turned their heads to leer at me, looked up from their maps to mock me. Eventually it felt like everyone was watching me, surrounding me, judging me. I was frozen with fear at first, unsure of what to do, until I felt a rush of paranoia creep in, and had the sudden urge to flee.

Like Peter two thousand years before me, I followed the ancient road back into Rome, marching—running, almost—to meet my fate.

CHAPTER FIFTEEN

"How was your trip to Jerusalem?" I asked.

Uri and I were standing in front of the restored crypt of Saint Sebastian, a Roman soldier and saint, in the catacombs underneath the small basilica that bears his name. Uri had called me the night before, telling me he was back in Rome, and wanted to meet me here the following morning.

"It was...uneventful," he said, not peeling his eyes from the stone box that housed the remains of the Christian soldier martyred by Emperor Diocletian in A.D. 288.

We were in one of the smallest underground Christian cemeteries, originally called *ad catacumbas*—loosely translated as "near the hollows" and so named because of the rock quarries located nearby. Catacumbas later became *catacomb*, a word that would come to describe any underground cemetery.

But this wasn't just any underground cemetery.

"The remains of Saints Peter and Paul were stored in this basilica for several decades for safe keeping during the years of Christian persecution," Uri said, finally looking at me with tired eyes.

It seems I would get no more information about Uri's trip back to Jerusalem. Whatever his business there, he returned less paranoid, it seemed to me, less on edge, if not less tired. Did his visit with Lev calm him down, ease his anxiety? If so, why was Lev just the opposite on the phone with me? Urgent, in a hurry, insisting that I was in danger?

Something didn't add up, but a sacred crypt didn't seem the right place to broach the subject.

I had to believe that Lev was okay, and that Uri would reveal himself in due time.

"Is that why you brought me here?" I asked.

"Yes, because of its supposed connection with Peter."

"Supposed?"

"There is no real archeological evidence placing Peter's or Paul's remains here, other than ancient graffiti invoking the two saints for aid and protection."

"Another dead end," I whispered.

"No," Uri said firmly. "These catacombs, this basilica, the basilica of John Lateran, Saint Peter's....they all serve a purpose."

"Which is?"

Uri paused, then took my hand. "Come with me."

He led me through dark, narrow tunnels of stone, punctuated by niches in the wall that once held bodies. We occasionally had to turn sideways to accommodate oncoming tourists and shimmy past outcroppings of rock. Finally we came to a small chamber that branched off from the main walkway, with empty stone niches on three sides of us. Uri stopped and looked over my shoulder before speaking.

"Mara, evidence placing Peter's death in Jerusalem may be weak, but what does it matter to the faithful?" He motioned to the dozen or so stone niches. "Many important Christians are buried down here, including Popes. This is a city of sacred bones!"

"And?" I said, unsure what Uri was hinting at.

"Just being near these relics that they can identify with is enough for Christians to maintain their faith."

"So how does that help me, my novel, our mission? The only relic or concrete evidence I have to plead my case for Peter's burial in Jerusalem is an ossuary with his name on it. That's hardly enough to convince people."

"Yes, but what solid evidence have I presented so far that places Peter in *Rome* at the time of his burial?"

I thought about this a moment. "None. Yet."

"That's right. It's *tradition* that keeps people going. The belief that Peter might be buried in Rome, that it could be true, is enough for Christians."

"Christians believe Peter was martyred and buried in Rome so it might as well be true. Is that what you're saying?"

Uri nodded.

"Again, I'm not seeing how that's going to help me."

"Remember I said that places like this, like Saint John Lateran, like Saint Peter's, serve a purpose. And that is the concept of proximity building faith."

"The lack of archeological evidence doesn't weaken Christians' belief. It's simply being near what they think is true that keeps their faith alive."

"Yes. Now you understand."

"Fine, but readers aren't going to believe Peter is buried in Jerusalem just because I told them so. As for me, being near concrete evidence, seeing tangible objects, is what builds my faith. Not immeasurable concepts."

"I'm afraid we haven't found any more proof yet placing Peter in Jerusalem at the time of his burial."

"Other than the ossuary," I said, sighing. "So what are you suggesting? That I give up?"

"Of course not," Uri said, taking both my hands in his. It was the first time he'd shown affection since his return from Jerusalem. My hands tensed up and he gripped me tighter. "I'm suggesting that you approach your novel in a different way."

I looked down at our hands intertwined. "I don't have concrete, tangible evidence, so I have to somehow sell readers on the immeasurable concept that Peter was buried in Jerusalem. How the hell am I going to do that?"

"It can partially be achieved by presenting the lack of concrete, tangible evidence placing Peter in *Rome* at the time of his burial."

"I don't know," I whispered, more to myself than to Uri. "Maybe he's right."

"Who?"

"Giovanni. I think he believes I'm on a fool's mission. Maybe he's right."

"When did Giovanni say that?"

"I went to see him while you were in Jerusalem."

"Mara yakiri," Uri said, stepping closer to me. "I'm sorry I left you alone."

"I wasn't alone, I was surrounded by people. It gave me a chance to see more of the city, and I had a nice visit with Giovanni."

"What did he say?"

"He was very kind in not discouraging our mission." I looked at Uri, at his chiseled face and brown eyes. Then I sighed heavily and took a leap of faith. "And he said to give you time...that your feelings for me would reveal themselves in good time."

Uri's hands loosened inside mine. "You discussed our relationship with Giovanni?"

"He brought it up. He's very intuitive."

Uri smiled and whispered, "Yes he is." Then he squeezed my hands tighter. "And he's right."

"About what?"

"Remember what we just discussed? That proximity builds faith?"

"Of course."

"Other than the two days I spent in Jerusalem, I have been by your side this whole time."

"I know."

"That proximity should've built your faith that I love you."

I felt a twinge in my belly, the kind that precipitates a moment of passion.

"Do you have faith that I love you?" Uri continued. "Do you believe that I love you?"

"Faith is a powerful thing, Uri. But it's not always enough. At least not for me..."

He took a step forward, kissed my cheek and whispered, "What will it take for you to believe?"

I could feel his breath on my face, feel his closeness. "Concrete, tangible evidence," I whispered back.

Uri's eyes searched mine. Finally, he said, "I love you, Mara yakiri."

Then he wrapped his arms around me and kissed me—deeply, passionately, and without abandon.

Breathless, and with my eyes still closed, I whispered, "About damn time."

Uri laughed softly. "Now do you believe?"

"Now I believe."

"There is so much more I want you to see."

Finally, I opened my eyes.

"I want you to show me everything."

CHAPTER SIXTEEN

I woke to the sound of the phone ringing. I was in my hotel room, under the covers, naked.

"Don't get that," Uri said, his eyes still closed.

I propped myself up on one elbow and scanned his naked torso. "But it might be important."

"I doubt it." He opened his eyes and smiled. "Good morning, Mara yakiri."

I bent down and kissed him, deciding that whoever was calling could leave a message.

Uri and I had spent the rest of the day after our visit to the catacombs as tourists. Having told Uri I needed a break from our mission, and, having had my fill of architecture, I requested we go somewhere completely disassociated with biblical history. Uri took me to the Villa Borghese, where we trolled the art museums and strolled arm and arm through the 19th century English-style landscaped garden. Then, after a romantic, candlelit dinner, we retired to my hotel room.

"So what's on the agenda today, professor?" I said, standing and preparing to get in the shower.

Uri watched me from the bed, one eye open. "Remember yesterday when I said there was so much I wanted you to see?" he asked.

I nodded. "And I said I wanted you to show me everything..."

"It starts today," he said, that familiar twinkle in his eye. "And it culminates tonight. Tonight will be a very special night, indeed."

CHAPTER SEVENTEEN

A music festival at an open-air amphitheatre. A stroll through the Roman Forum along the Via Sacra, the main street of ancient Rome. A sunset boat tour up the Tiber River. A romantic candlelit dinner.

Uri had the whole day planned, and by the time we sank into a corner booth for that candlelit dinner, I was giddy with exhaustion and overwhelmed with passion and hungry for more.

It still felt like a dream—my romance with Uri. It was what I had been naively hoping for for almost two years, starting soon after our first adventure in Jerusalem. At first I was singularly focused on finding the correlation between the Talpiot tomb and Jesus, and weaving that into a controversial thriller of a novel that would re-invent my career. But as the days ticked by and I got to know Uri better as well as the country he called home, priorities changed. Rather, *dreams* changed. My interest in proving an ancient burial cave was the final resting place of Jesus also turned into a quest to prove if Jerusalem was meant to be my new home...with Uri.

And while I never did prove if the Talpiot tomb was the final resting place of Jesus, I did manage to wrestle a best-selling novel out of it. The same couldn't be said of a relationship with Uri. He stayed in Jerusalem and I went home to Philadelphia and there we lived separate lives and barely stayed in touch.

Fate had flipped a coin. Career or love, which would it be? I was destined to have one but not the other.

That time around, the coin had landed on career.

Now, two years and many blissful nights later, I felt I didn't have to choose anymore. I had time and luck and, possibly, fate on my side. I could focus on both endeavors: write a sequel to the best-selling novel that put my career back on the map, and nurture a relationship that would put my love life back on the map. I could do both successfully and finally feel like I could have it all.

My second trip to Rome hadn't started out well, and I had been close to giving up hope for a relationship with Uri and in finishing our mission. I was close to telling Jenny she'd been right.

Then somehow, some way, fate intervened. But...

But if the relationship were to last, how could we possibly make it work?

"What are we going to do, Uri?" I had asked that night over dinner.

"We'll eat lots of food and drink lots of wine, and then go for a night-time stroll and—"

"No. That's not what I meant."

Uri looked at me with a puzzled look but tenderness in his eyes that suggested he knew I needed him to be serious.

"You live in Jerusalem, I live in Philadelphia..."

He paused before answering. "I think it's best we focus on our mission first."

"And then what?"

"And then....we see what happens and plan from there."

"Do you miss Jerusalem? Are you anxious to get back?"

"Of course," Uri said, taking my hand in his. "But I made a commitment to you. We have so much more to see, things to discover, a mystery to solve..."

"What about your work? You've made a commitment to the university as well."

Uri averted my eyes and didn't answer.

"It seems the brief trip back to Jerusalem changed you," I continued.

He snapped his head up. "How do you mean?"

"You seem...refreshed...less anxious, less stressed-out, maybe?"

He seemed relived by my answer. "Yes, I feel refreshed. The trip home has done me good."

Uri Nevon may have seemed less anxious, less on-edge, and he may have confessed his love for me, but he was no less guarded with his answers. He still seemed reluctant to confess what he was truly thinking. There was still a hesitancy about him, the source of which I couldn't put my finger on. I downed the rest of my red wine and proceeded with full guns blazing.

"Why did you go back to Jerusalem?" I asked.

"It is the end of the semester. I had students to meet with. Final exams to grade..."

"And?"

"I spent two days catching up at the university and hopped right back on a plane."

"Don't forget you went to see Lev," I blurted out. I pinched my eyes and hoped what I'd heard was the voice in my head, that I hadn't actually verbalized it.

But I had.

"Shit," I said, drawing out the word.

"How...how did you know that?" he asked, his face solemn.

I paused a moment, deciding how to proceed. "I called him."

"With what intention?" He seemed angered.

"I was worried about you. You seemed distant in the days leading up to your return to Jerusalem. I thought something might be going on, maybe something I said or did. So I called Lev."

"Why didn't you ask me directly?"

"You wouldn't have told me. In fact, you didn't tell me why you were returning to Jerusalem in the first place. You were very cryptic about the whole trip."

Uri paused. "I'm sorry about that..." Then, "You thought Lev would have insight?"

"I don't know!" I said. "I thought maybe you had bumped into him, and if so, I wanted to see if you seemed different to him, too."

I was dangerously close to betraying Lev's trust. He'd called me in a panic to make sure I was okay, and then begged me not to tell Uri he'd called me. But Lev seemed to be in danger, and I thought Uri's return to Jerusalem might have something to do with it. I desperately wanted to know what was going on. If our mission in Rome was jeopardizing either of them, I had to know. I couldn't let them sacrifice their lives for me again. So I told a white lie and said I called Lev, instead of the other way around.

Then an idea hit me. It would require another white lie, but it would push the direction of the conversation away from Lev.

"I thought maybe...you went back to see Ziva."

His eyes widened as if in disbelief. Just then the waiter arrived with our food. Uri waited for him to leave before continuing. He leaned forward and whispered, "She is a part of my past."

A pang of guilt hit me in the gut. "Please understand. I just needed to make sure."

"I love you, Mara. You must know that."

"I do now. But I didn't then." Then, smiling, I said, "Took you long enough."

Uri looked coy, then his expression turned to concern. "I didn't want feelings to endanger—compromise—our mission."

"I understand that. I have the same concern. But you're the reason I am achieving my goal in the first place. If it weren't for you, the first book wouldn't even exist. And without you, there'd be no second book."

"I hope you still feel that way when this is all over..."

"Of course I will."

Of course I would feel the same about Uri when our adventure was over. The gratitude, the respect, the admiration, the love... They would remain unchanged, I felt, forever.

But what I felt changing, as we dug deeper inside the life of Saint Peter, were my feelings about our mission in Rome. There was no concrete evidence of Peter's burial in Jerusalem. Nothing Uri said or did could change that. You can't change history. He must know and understand that better than anyone.

So maybe that was the reason for Uri's sudden sadness. Perhaps he felt it, too. The heavy hand of fate intervening. That no matter what he did, he couldn't change the past.

Fate was yet again poised to flip a coin, and this time perhaps we were destined for each other, and our mission in Rome—our chance to prove that Peter was buried in Jerusalem—was doomed to failure.

CHAPTER EIGHTEEN

U ri promised "a very special night," then made a hasty retreat after dinner. He said he'd be in touch but didn't say when. I had no choice but to retreat to my room and wait for further instructions.

Which was okay, because the time alone would allow me to do some research. And my top priority was learning more about the two groups that seemed to be the center of the Saint Peter mystery: the Ordo Fratrum Minorum, or the Order of Friars Minor, and the smaller group of friars contained therein, the Custody of the Holy Land.

I knew a little about the Custody of the Holy Land from the conversation Uri and Lev had in Lev's store, and from my own conversation with Giovanni. Most notably, that they were the "guardians" of Christendom's holy places and relics—including the Church of the Flagellation where Uri and I had had our run-in with Benjamin and his henchmen.

The Franciscan movement as a whole dates back to the time of Francis of Assisi in the 13th century. Undoubtedly one of the most popular saints in the history of the Church, Francis grew up in a wealthy household as the son of a successful fabric merchant. Over the years he worked his way up in his father's business, but somewhere along the way he began to eschew his privileged life in favor of a more simple life—a life free of political strife, free from the power of possessions and the chains of consumerism, a life lived according to the gospel.

From this, a movement was born, the Franciscan Order of Friars, a ministry less familiar than the man for whom the movement was named.

Over time the movement branched out from its small and humble beginnings in Assisi, Italy, to the four corners of the then-known world. The mission at first was not conversion, possession or conquest, but simply access—gaining the trust and acceptance of the populace so they could gain access to sanctuaries for worship. Then, once ensconced among the people, and having gained the right to worship their way, the Franciscan Order would be recognized as a suitable alternative to the Catholic Church and all its corruption and cronyism.

Ironic, given that the Franciscans were a *part* of the Catholic Church. In effect, they sought to challenge the Church while proclaiming allegiance to it at the same time.

The friars had divided the known world into provinces, which were further broken down into "custodies," settlements the friars established that were usually centered around principle geographic areas of known religious activities: Italy and other areas around the western Mediterranean; Egypt, Israel, Lebanon and other areas of the eastern Mediterranean; and further outposts including Russia, Tibet, and China.

The most important custody to the friars formed an arc around the eastern Mediterranean. It included Egypt to the west, Israel, Jordan, Lebanon and Syria to the northeast, and wrapped around westward to Turkey and Greece. Because this area of the world contained the lands of the Bible, and included the homeland of Jesus, this custody was named *The Custody of the Holy Land*.

Giovanni had said the Ordo Fratrum Minorum was the most prominent group of Franciscans, and it is this group that people are usually referring to when they say "Franciscan."

And it was this group that was in control of the ossuary of Saint Peter. So if I wanted to see the ossuary again, or any other Saint Peter relic they might have in their possession, I'd have to find a way to win them over.

But first I'd have to find them.

Little did I know they'd find *me* first.

My phone buzzed on the bed next to me and I glanced over at the display.

Saint Peter's Square. Tonight. 10 p.m.

The text from Uri startled me. I was deep in thought about the Custody of the Holy Land, wondering if they should play a role in the new novel I was writing. They were powerful. They were members of the Catholic Church. And no doubt they were hiding secrets. I didn't have a protagonist yet, and this group was proving to be a worthy candidate.

I texted back "10-4" to let Uri know I was on board with whatever adventure he had planned next, and followed it with another text that simply stated, "love you."

As I packed up my laptop and slipped into a light jacket, my phone buzzed two more times.

Plans confirmed.

Love you too.

CHAPTER NINETEEN

S oft, yellowish light illuminated the square and bounced off the cobblestones, bathing Saint Peter's Square in an ethereal glow. How much larger the square seemed at night, nearly emptied of tourists and devoid of sound.

A few people milled about: young lovers on moonlit strolls, photographers, locals simply passing through, a female writer on a mission....

....and Dr. Giovanni Maderno.

I saw him as I approached the obelisk in the middle of the square. He stood off to the right side of it, and as I turned to make sure it was him he waved emphatically and called out to me.

"Mara, over here!"

"Giovanni, what are you doing here?"

The professor looked at me impishly.

"What has Uri put you up to this time?" I asked.

He shrugged as if to proclaim innocence. "He needed my help, so here I am."

"And where is that little rascal?" I asked, looking around the square.

Just then I saw Uri to my left, emerging from behind the obelisk.

Giovanni gave me a funny look. "Little rascal...?" he mouthed at me as Uri approached us.

"Thank you so very much for agreeing to this," Uri addressed Giovanni.

Giovanni bowed in a show of loyalty.

"Agreeing to what?" I asked.

Uri looked at me playfully. "It's a surprise."

"You promised me a special night," I said, teasingly.

"And you'll get it."

"There was no mention of surprises."

"You should have expected it."

"Of course I should have."

Uri shrugged. "Surprise!"

I glanced at Giovanni, who was looking at each of us in turn as we spoke, smiling.

Uri started to walk through the square towards the basilica, beckoning us both to follow. Giovanni stood for a moment, speechless, his mouth open as if waiting for words to emerge. "What was that?" he whispered to me as we started to walk behind Uri.

"What was what?"

"Something is happening between you..."

"You were right all along, professor."

"You mean...?" He motioned between Uri and me with an index finger. I nodded.

"I told you!" he said, clapping his hands together. "Didn't I tell you it was amore?"

Uri craned his head to the side as he walked and called out to us. "What are you two doing back there?"

"Nothing!" I called out, motioning to Giovanni for us to catch up.

"I'm so glad, signora!" Giovanni whispered as we bridged the gap a few paces behind Uri. Then, more to himself he whispered, "I hope I'm invited to the wedding."

"Let's not get ahead of ourselves," I said as the three of us climbed the steps and approached the main entrance, the Door of the Sacraments, the door located to the right of the central door.

"Of course," Giovanni said. "First things first, no?" He looked at Uri, who nodded at him. "Enjoy your evening," Giovanni said to each of us, kissed me on the cheek, shook Uri's hand, then pushed open the heavy door and disappeared from sight.

"Where's he going?" I asked. Uri took my hand firmly as if to hold me in place, to keep me from following him.

"Give him a few minutes," was Uri's answer.

Those few minutes felt like hours. Uri wouldn't tell me what was going on and in fact remained mostly silent with a coy smile on his face. Finally he looked at his watch and announced, "It's time."

Uri led me through the Door of the Sacraments into the nave. We were all alone inside the large and beautiful basilica. Without a word we walked down the center aisle until we came upon the entrance to Saint Peter's tomb in front of the papal altar. I craned my neck to look up at Bernini's Baldacchino, a huge slab of greek marble sculpted to look like a canopy that towers above the altar, then down at the double ramp of stairs that descends to what some believe is the true heart of the basilica, Saint Peter's tomb.

Or the supposed tomb of Saint Peter.

I looked over at Uri, who was looking at me, smiling.

"Are we going down there?" I asked, pointing.

Uri nodded. "You are about to see what so few people have seen in thousands of years. Areas beneath the basilica not open to the public and held in such secret that only high-ranking church members can gain access."

Then he paused, and I felt a tingle of anticipation arise in my stomach.

"Are you ready?" he asked.

CHAPTER TWENTY

Twenty minutes later I found myself in the grottoes beneath Saint Peter's Basilica, walking through a labyrinthine maze of tunnels surrounded by tombs and sarcophagi.

A virtual necropolis, city of the dead.

But what I saw surprised me. This wasn't the dark, damp dungeon-like cave I was expecting. What I encountered were brightly lit hallways with stark white walls and travertine floors. Ornately decorated chapel rooms with gilded gold ceilings and colorfully frescoed walls. And well-maintained rooms adorned with religious iconography for pilgrims to sit and pray.

Surrounded by such color and beauty I would have hardly guessed I was underground.

But I was, with Uri at my side, and we had the whole place to ourselves. We spent time exploring each hallway, each chapel, each niche and each stone tomb, learning more about this city of the dead and its inhabitants. Along the way we saw tombs of kings and queens, stone statues of saints and popes, and galleries filled with religious icons and iconography.

After awhile I grew restless. These areas were great in their own right, but all were obviously open to the public. Uri said we'd be seeing areas off-limits to tourists, accessible to only high-ranking church officials. Those are the areas I wanted to see. I was sure it was in some hidden corner of the grottoes, hidden away from prying eyes, where I'd find Saint Peter.

"Where is he?" I finally asked.

Uri must've sensed my impatience and knew I was ready to move on. He motioned me forward, through a maze of hallways we hadn't been down yet, arched alleyways paved with gold whose entrances had been blocked by padlocked gates but now stood open. I sensed we were going deeper into the bowels of the necropolis, into sensitive areas with long-held secrets.

Suddenly we made a hard left into a small room, highly decorated with bronze and gold and richly-colored mosaics and three marble steps leading up to an altar. This was no ordinary room, I thought as I looked around the room. The room was narrow but deep and it seemed no surface was left unadorned by paint or a precious metal.

"The so-called gem of the Vatican grottoes," Uri said, spinning around to take in all the details. "The Chapel of Saint Peter."

I remained silent, continuing to take it all in.

"This chapel is part of the original basilica built by Emperor Constantine in the fourth century," Uri continued, "and is the only part of that ancient basilica to have preserved its original function."

With this announcement I sank into one of the small wooden benches, overwhelmed by the thought that for more than a millennia, oaths to Saint Peter were sworn in this tiny, ancient room by pilgrims and popes alike.

"Did it look like this back then?" I said.

"No. Pope Clement VIII commissioned for it to be richly decorated for his Great Jubilee in 1600. He also enlarged the room, vaulted the ceiling and raised the altar. So the way you see it now is how it's looked for more than four hundred years. Because of his renovations, the room was named the Clementine Chapel in his honor."

"It's obviously still used to this day."

"Yes," he confirmed, standing over me now.

"Open to the public."

Uri smirked, knowing what I was hinting at. "Mara, don't be disappointed. This is the original altar of the original basilica from antiquity, nearly fifteen hundred years old." It is believed that Peter was crucified on this *very spot*, and that his blood soaked the earth on which we stand..."

"I appreciate your bringing me here," I said, standing to face Uri.

"Peter's death here was the inspiration for Constantine to build this chapel," Uri continued, as if he hadn't heard me. "This is ground zero for the Peter movement."

"I guess I was just expecting...*more*..."

Just then Uri's cell phone chirped, indicating he'd received a text message. He scanned the message and, with quick fingers and a solemn face, typed a reply.

"Everything okay?" I asked.

"Yes, just Giovanni..."

I could always tell when Uri was hiding the truth. Sometimes there was the tell-tale sign of refusing to make eye contact. But with him, it was usually something else: The way his eyes pinched up ever so slightly into a squint, as if hit by light. He had the same look on his face at the Mamertine Prison, when I asked why he seemed spooked by his own shadow. And he looked the same the day we saw the shards of Saint Peter's ossuary, while we were speaking to the security guard. And he was doing it now, after I'd asked him if something was the matter.

"Where is he, by the way?" I asked. "I'd like to thank him. Obviously he had something to do with our after-hours admittance."

"He will be back later, after we've left," Uri said, finally meeting my gaze.

"To lock up?"

"Yes. Giovanni has....special connections...that allow him certain privileges."

"He's best friends with the Pope?" I said, trying to cut the tension that had suddenly arisen in the room. I may have made the comment in jest, but in reality something about Uri's choice of words startled me.

Special connections?

Up until now I'd known Giovanni as a run-on-the-mill Roman, albeit a smart, cultured man with a passion for architecture. He was a father figure to me, someone who was always quick to dole out advice and make poignant observations right when it seemed I needed it the most. I hadn't had someone like that in my life since my father died.

So if Giovanni had a hidden agenda, or belonged to some shady, clandestine group...well, I didn't think I could handle that truth.

"So you want more?" Uri asked, ignoring my comment about Giovanni knowing the Pope. "Then let me show you the real reason you're here."

CHAPTER TWENTY-ONE

U ri led me through an entranceway next to the Clementine Chapel. Walking forty feet led us into a maze of ancient catacombs, with low archways, large mausoleums, and half-walls of crumbling brick, all on a narrow path that seemed to wind on forever.

As we shuffled along in the near-dark, millennia year old dirt crunching beneath our feet, I thought, *This* is what I'd expected to see and experience. It felt like we were walking through the streets of a dark, dreary city. Except this city was filled with dead people.

"This is the Vatican necropolis," Uri explained as we walked. Then he smirked at me. "Off limits to the public."

"What keeps people from finding their way here from the Chapel of Saint Peter?" I looked back in the direction we'd come from. "There's no gate or blockade..."

"Guards," Uri said, as if the answer was obvious.

"Right."

"Anyway," Uri continued, "most of this pre-dates Constantine."

"Pre-Christian, in other words," I said, struggling to keep my balance navigating through the narrow alley, over rock piles and around outcroppings of marble and plaster.

The air was warm and humid and beads of sweat started to form at the nape of my neck. I dabbed at them with a handkerchief and kept walking.

"Precisely," Uri said, then motioned me inside a rock-hewn tomb. "Look at this." He pointed to a wall mosaic featuring a scene from Greek mythology: the god Dionysus with a young satyr at his feet.

"But there are traces of Christianity as well," Uri said, leading me out of that tomb into an adjacent tomb. "Like this." He pointed at a bas-relief carving on the wall of the tomb of a woman drawing water from a well surrounded by doves, an olive branch above her head.

Etched on the stone were the Latin words "dormit in pace": *rest in peace.*

"Who are all these people?" I asked as we started walking again, to where, I didn't know yet. Uri was leading the way and we continued on in a straight line, past simple rock tombs with niches for bodies, and mosaic- and paint-filled rooms of grandeur depicting scenes of animals and plants and flowers and fruit.

"Excavations tell us that most of them were commoners, not nobles," Uri said, craning his head to one side to speak as I walked behind.

"Based on all the lavish decorations and fine materials you'd think they were all kings and queens."

"Poor in status, perhaps, but not in means."

"What do you mean?"

"These were working-class merchants and their family members," Uri said. There was a spring to his step now, as if he was on a mission—in a hurry, really—to get somewhere. "They came from modest backgrounds but their craftsmanship gave them able economic opportunities. All that commerce allowed them to build elegant tombs for themselves and their relatives."

"How long ago are we talking?" I asked, my breathing becoming short and shallow.

"Second century A.D."

"So this whole complex was here before the basilica above us."

Uri craned his head back again, and I could hear his labored breathing. "It's important to keep in mind that this was a public burial ground outside of the city walls. Two hundred years later, when Constantine decided to build a church devoted to Saint Peter, the land was still in use. He believed Saint Peter was buried in this necropolis because of its proximity to where Peter was supposedly martyred."

"So he built his church directly on top of a graveyard?" I asked incredulously.

Uri turned around and wordlessly shrugged as if to say, *don't shoot the messenger*.

"That's like building a house on top of a cemetery. Didn't he care about protecting all this history, not to mention desecrating all the tombs?"

"That I don't know," Uri said, starting to walk again. "What I do know is that he cared about preserving the legacy of Saint Peter. So while portions of the necropolis were inevitably tampered with, filled with soil and construction materials, he managed to preserve the tomb of Saint Peter."

Then Uri abruptly stopped, and we were standing in what appeared to be an open courtyard.

"So what happened to this necropolis when Constantine's basilica was built?" I asked.

"It ceased being used. It disappeared, literally and fugitively."

"For how long?"

"Nearly thirteen hundred years, until the present-day basilica was built. But it wasn't until the twentieth century that *he* was found." Uri pointed over his shoulder.

I didn't get Uri's meaning at first, until I took a few steps toward the niche and the graffiti-covered wall behind it. "You mean...?"

Uri nodded. "Welcome to the tomb of Saint Peter."

CHAPTER TWENTY-TWO

The wall behind the niche in front of me was littered with crude etchings, ancient inscriptions, mostly in Greek, running in all directions, some criss-crossing each other. They were the markings of the faithful, memorials to deceased friends and relatives, wishes for salvation, expressions of gratitude, hopes for peace.

Uri said many such inscription-filled walls exist in antiquity, and it usually marks the spot where religious figures lie, saints and popes and martyrs alike.

But this plaster wall, the so-called "Red" wall because it was once covered with red paint, was different from other Christian graffiti sites. The sheer volume of inscriptions and etchings marked this as a place of extreme importance, a place venerated for hundreds of years by the faithful.

Uri motioned to one inscription in particular, and I stepped closer and peered through the niche to look at it.

"Petros Eni," Uri said. "Greek for 'Peter is here.'"

Just then Uri's phoned buzzed. He looked at the text message and his mouth twitched, as if attempting to hide a frown.

"This is the place many believe Saint Peter's bones were found," he continued, still holding his phone in his hand, "and remain to this day."

Uri pointed to a small opening in the graffiti wall. "This hole was completely encased in marble when it was found. Inside the hole excavators found a box of bones..."

Uri's phone buzzed again and he looked at the new text message. This time he didn't attempt to hide his distress. "It's almost time to go."

"What about the bones?" I asked, momentarily forgetting Uri's sudden sense of urgency.

"They were found to belong to a man in his sixties or seventies, roughly the age Peter was when he died." Uri looked nervous, anxious, on-edge, as he had so many times throughout our journey. "And the bones had traces of purple and gold thread, further indicating that he was a man of some importance."

"Great, more nails in my coffin," I whispered.

Uri looked at his watch. "The 'Peter is here' inscription could mean nothing, Mara. Remember what I said about proximity breeding belief..."

"Yes, I remember," I said, still not convinced we were any closer to debunking the belief that Peter was buried in Rome.

"This inscription could've been scribbled by someone who wants to believe Saint Peter was buried here. Or the inscription could've been misinterpreted. We know from exploring the Talpiot tomb that paleographers differ in their interpretations of ancient languages."

"Okay, but the Greek language hasn't changed much in thousands of years. Aramaic, the language found on first-century bone boxes and in Jewish tombs, is dead."

Uri placed his hand on the small of my back as if to lead me out of the tomb. "Let's discuss this on the way out."

"We're leaving?"

"I'm afraid we must."

"Why the sudden hurry?" I asked, standing my ground. "Who texted you? Was it Giovanni again?"

Uri nodded and said nothing.

"What's going on?"

"I just think it's best if we...wrap things up..."

"But we just got here..."

"There's nothing left to see."

"Are you serious? There's plenty left to see."

Uri's phone buzzed a third time. He looked me in the eye. "Do you trust me?"

"Of course I do."

He held his phone up for me to read three text messages from Giovanni:

Time's up

Leave now

Can't guarantee safety

"I—I thought Giovanni arranged all this..." I stuttered. "Are we going to get in trouble?"

"I'll explain later, I promise," Uri said. "But we need to go. Now."

With that, and without further questioning from me or explanation from him, I submitted to Uri's warning. We retraced our steps, through the ancient necropolis thirty feet underground, up through the more recent hallways of the grottoes, and finally up to the ground level of the basilica.

By the time we made our way back outside to Saint Peter's Square we were both winded and woozy and pained in our own ways: Uri for fear that we'd get in trouble for what we'd just done, and me for having come no closer to proving that Saint Peter was buried in Jerusalem.

It had been a special night, all right. Just not the kind of special I'd imagined.

CHAPTER TWENTY-THREE

I woke up alone with nothing but a dull headache for company. I looked around the room in a daze and my eyes finally settled on the empty bottle of wine on the night stand.

I'd discovered the reason for the hangover but had to try harder to come up with the reason why I had spent the night alone.

Slowly it all came back to me as I stepped into the shower. After our interrupted mission last evening I couldn't shake the feeling that Uri was hiding something. He was definitely hiding something, for no other reason, I was sure, than to protect me. Whatever it was had to be a doozy, because Giovanni was most insistent that we leave the basilica for our own safety's sake.

I confronted Uri as we taxied through the streets of Rome en route back to my hotel. He walked me to my room, where an argument ensued. I accused him of lying, he accused me of not being able to let things be. I insisted that I didn't need protecting, that whatever the truth was I could handle it, that I didn't want this mission—and its complications—to interfere with our relationship. He said it was too late, that that had already happened. When I probed him for an explanation, he only said that his passion always had a way of getting himself—and the ones he loved—in trouble.

He said he needed a day to think things over. I thought he was breaking up with me. He said he wasn't, that he loved me and wanted us to be together, but that he thought we needed a day apart to really think about our mission in Rome.

What was our goal in Rome? he'd asked. Had we gotten any closer to achieving that goal? Would I be disappointed if I didn't achieve that goal? If he wasn't able to help me achieve my goal? Would I be okay with simply walking away?

He wanted me to think about those questions for a day, but only a day, because he said he couldn't be away from me for longer than that.

It was agreed we'd meet for dinner the next night and start answering those questions together.

Then he said he needed to go, and I thought he should go, so I watched him walk away, down the hallway, around the corner and out of site. He'd paused once or twice, turning his head to the side as if to see if I was still there.

Then I ordered a bottle of wine from room service to get over the pain of our first argument and also to celebrate getting it the hell out of the way.

I dried my hair and got dressed, wondering where I should go and what I should do for the day. I had decided to visit the Coliseum and was just reviewing a map when my cell phone rang. The caller I.D. read private and I didn't recognize the number.

"Hello?"

"Hello, Mara." The voice was steady and firm, and maybe a little menacing. I paused a moment, attempting to identify it.

"Ben?"

"Surprised to hear from me?"

"A little. How'd you get my number?"

"I'm a police officer," he said, as if that was enough of an explanation.

"What can I do for you?"

"I've been meaning to call you..."

"About what?"

When he paused I said, "Is this about Lev? Is he OK?"

"Why wouldn't he be? He's not why I'm calling."

"Am I in trouble?" I said, half-jokingly. "Are you going to hold me at gunpoint and blind-fold me again?"

"That was the guard's idea, not mine."

"Holding me at gun point or blind-folding me?"

"The museum staff insisted I blind-fold you. And neither I nor my men held anyone at gun point."

"Yes, I realize that. I was trying to make a point."

"Taken," he said. "And that is actually why I'm calling. I want to apologize for being....*rough*...on you and Uri."

"No need. You were just doing your job."

"Well, tempers were starting to flare and emotions were starting to show and given Uri's past...."

I wondered whose temper and emotions he was talking about. Uri seemed calm as usual that day. The security guard had gotten a little testy, and I knew I'd given Ben some lip about seeing the ossuary so if anything I should be apologizing to him. And Ben might've seemed a little angry at first, and suspicious of Uri and his intentions which I could understand. But when Ben hung up the phone with his mysterious caller suddenly his demeanor changed—he was calm and cooperative and willing to compromise. Something about that didn't sit right with me.

And now the sudden mea culpa. That didn't seem like something Ben would do. Something seemed off.

"No need to worry, Ben. Water under the bridge."

"So how's your little mission going?"

"What do you know about it?"

"Something to do with Saint Peter. That's all I know... And that you think the ossuary held at the Church of the Flagellation belonged to him."

"It does," I said matter-of-factly, and Ben laughed.

"What evidence do you have proving that?"

"It's the only ossuary in existence with the names Simon and Jonah on it."

"Are there no other Simons in the world with fathers named Jonah?" Ben asked, not waiting for me to answer before asking another question. "What else do you have?"

"There is no other ossuary in the world like this one," I said, starting to get agitated. "It was found at Dominus Flevit, an area Jesus and his apostles are known to have spent time, in a burial site known to be the final resting place of many first-century Jews and followers of Jesus."

"Can I presume, then, that you are attempting to prove Saint Peter is not buried in Rome, but in Jerusalem?"

"Can I presume you are interrogating me again?"

Ben chuckled. "My apologies, Miss Beltane. I find it hard sometimes to turn off the policeman side of me."

I paused, attempting to regain my composure. What was it about this guy that got under my skin? Why did he always seem to have the upper hand?

"What if I *was* trying to prove Saint Peter was buried in Jerusalem?" I asked.

"I would say good luck...and be careful..."

"Is that a warning?"

Ben paused. "Let's call it a friendly suggestion."

"Why do you care? We're not in your jurisdiction. If Uri's up to his old tricks, which you seem to think he is, it's not your problem."

"Curiosity, I suppose. To see if you can pull it off."

"And? What do you think of our odds?"

"Oh, I don't know... It partially depends on the type of help you're receiving."

I thought about his comment a minute. "Lev's not involved, if that's what you're insinuating."

"I'm not insinuating anything. I'm a police officer, remember?"

"Yes, so you keep saying."

"And I know Lev's not involved because I've asked him."

"You have?"

"You thought I wouldn't? He's my nephew, Miss Beltane. I'm concerned about his well being."

"And you're not concerned about mine or Uri's?"

"I called you, didn't I? Even though you're *not my problem...*"

His words felt like a dagger slice to the cheek. I wanted to hang up on him, but we'd broached the subject of Lev. I wanted to make sure he was okay, and I didn't want Ben to know about Lev's frantic phone call to me.

"What did Lev say?" I asked.

"That he has no involvement in your mission."

"That's true. He doesn't."

"And we talked about his studies and the store and Sarah."

"Sarah?"

"His girlfriend."

"He mentioned he had a girlfriend. How long have they been dating?"

"Several months. They met at university. She's actually one of Dr. Nevon's students. They seem very happy. We have them over for dinner often."

By *we* I assumed he meant himself and Ziva. It seemed inevitable that she would eventually come up in conversation, so I decided to rip off the band-aid, swallow my pride, and ask how his wife was doing.

"Ziva is well?"

"Oh, you know...she's good."

"Still teaching at Hebrew University?"

"Yes, and enjoying it." Then he cleared his throat. "We are actually...well, we're trying to have a baby."

"That's great," I said. "Good luck."

"It is stressful, you know? When one person wants children and the other doesn't?"

I was surprised by Ben's sudden revelation. Why was he telling me this intimate detail of his life? I hated myself for thinking so, but I couldn't help but think there was a hidden agenda in his statement.

"I'm too old, too set in my ways..." he continued.

"I was in the same situation with my ex-husband, Thomas," I said, deciding to share in return to see where the conversation would lead.

"Ah, then you understand! It's always hard when the wife wants children and the husband does not."

"Actually, for me it was the other way around. I was the one who didn't want children."

"That right?"

"Yes. And unfortunately that ended our marriage."

"Needless to say you won't be having children with Uri?" Ben asked.

That comment surprised and somewhat angered me.

"I won't be having children with anyone. That shipped has sailed."

"Understood."

"And what do you think is going on between me and Uri?"

"I assume you are a couple?"

"I thought police officers never assumed anything."

He was silent a moment. "You are right. My apologies. I was wrong to assume anything, even though I think I am correct."

"What evidence do you have?"

"The day at the Church of the Flagellation. Uri was always touching you in some way. His hand on your back. A palm on your shoulder...."

"Very observant," I said. "What else do you have?"

"The way he looks at you. Gentle and protective..."

I was silent, deciding if I should let Ben off the hook and reveal our relationship.

"So then, can I presume you are a couple?" he asked.

"What if we were?"

"I would say congratulations...and good luck..."

"Is that a warning?"

Ben paused. "Let's call it a friendly suggestion."

I hung up the phone with Ben with the same mixed emotions I always felt towards him. He had a way of revealing information about himself to make him seem sensitive and empathetic. But then in the next breath he was arrogant and presumptuous.

Perhaps Benjamin Schwarz was misunderstood and deserved the benefit of the doubt; maybe he truly was trying to bury the hatchet the only way he knew how. But maybe he was hiding his true self, and an unrevealed MO lay just beneath the surface.

Either way, I would continue to keep Ben at arm's length, and Uri the distance of a hairsbreadth.

CHAPTER TWENTY-FOUR

He had requested we meet at a different restaurant that night for dinner. So many wonderful places to eat in Rome, he'd said. Why frequent the same one over and over?

I'd agreed and never would've caught on to Uri's hidden agenda had it not been for his careless mistake that night. And to this day I swear his careless mistake was a blessing in disguise. Perhaps the hand of fate intervening again. Because had he not been so careless, and had I not been so persistent, things could've gone much worse than they did. Perhaps neither of us would've made it out of Rome...

Truth is, I betrayed him. But I felt I had to. It was the only way to discover the truth that Uri seemed so unwilling to reveal.

And as it turned out, Uri's mistake, followed by my betrayal, ushered in a series of events that would forever alter the course of our lives.

• • • •

I WAS TIPPED OFF THAT something was amiss the moment we met in front of the restaurant. He looked all around him as I approached and then again after kissing me hello. Then he requested a table close to the entrance but away from any windows.

The paranoia continued throughout the duration of our meal. He had trouble keeping eye contact. He rebuffed any attempt I made at affection. And his whole body trembled slightly as if he overtaken by cold.

Which was impossible because it was seventy degrees and dry, a most perfect evening.

So after a delicious meal filled with conversation that was pleasant but getting us nowhere, I'd had enough. We hadn't yet talked about our mission in Rome, what Uri had said he wanted to discuss over dinner...and we'd managed to avoid discussing our fight.

"Are we ever going to talk about what's going on?" I'd said after taking the last bite of pasta primavera.

After two weeks of bliss, traipsing through Rome with the man I loved, I'd almost forgotten about whatever had been troubling him.

Well, forgotten is the wrong word, because I hadn't forgotten it so much as I'd moved it to an area of my subconscious for safekeeping. I didn't want to forget it. I just wasn't ready to deal with it at the time. Uri had been calm and happy and his usual charming self those two weeks, wrapped up in our mission and our relationship and I hadn't wanted to ruin the mood.

Now, Uri's paranoia was suddenly rearing its ugly head again, so it seemed the perfect time to deal with the situation and get back to reality. Plus, he asked me to contemplate our reasons for being in Rome, our mission, such as it was. Perhaps it was time to discuss that, too.

"Sure. Let's talk," he said.

"Actually, can we discuss something else first?"

Uri looked at me with unblinking eyes, his smile slowly fading. He gulped down some wine, his hands still trembling. "Of course, Mara yakiri. What is on your mind?"

There are times when it's important to take your time getting to the truth in order to soften the blow. Uri was good at that. He'd talk to you for hours, making you feel relaxed and comfortable, and then choosing just the right moment to reveal the truth. There certainly was value to that method, and as human beings we have all, at some point in our lives, withheld a truth for another person's benefit. But sometimes we are guilty of withholding the truth until it's most suitable and advantageous for ourselves.

I wasn't about ready to do either.

Fact was, I'd been patient with Uri. Pushing had only made him retreat, so I'd taken Giovanni's suggestion and waited until Uri was ready to reveal his feelings for me. And my patience had paid off.

But now I felt there was much more at stake. We were no longer talking about feelings and emotions. We were talking about our *lives*. And I felt that whatever Uri wasn't telling me had the power to put our lives in danger.

"Why have you been so paranoid lately? Looking over your shoulder, jumpy when people approach? I know now that Giovanni is involved...are we in danger?"

Uri pursed his lips and thought a moment. "I...I don't want to lie to you, but I can't tell you the truth either."

I was taken aback by the statement. Usually Uri tells me that nothing is wrong, that everything will be okay and other such reassurances. But this time was different. His statement was so blunt and free of pretense that it felt like a warning. I had the sudden feeling that I was right—that our lives were indeed in danger.

I hadn't the words to continue so thankfully Uri spoke first.

"I'm always looking over my shoulder because as you can imagine what we are attempting to do is dangerous. I don't want a repeat of what happened in Jerusalem."

"Okay," I said, keeping my response short to encourage him to keep talking.

"...and because I'm pretty sure we're being followed."

My stomach lurched. "What?" I said, perhaps too loudly. I lowered my voice. "How can you know that?"

"I just do," Uri said, staring at the table. Then to himself he said, "This is starting to feel like Jerusalem all over again. It's probably already too late. I told myself—"

Then he cut himself off.

"You told yourself what?"

Uri continued to stare at the table and said nothing.

"Uri? What did you tell yourself?" I hissed through clenched teeth.

He looked up at me with desperate brown eyes. "I told myself when we parted in Jerusalem two years ago that I would always protect you..."

I furrowed my brows at him, confused by his statement. "But we didn't think we'd ever see each other again."

"I did," he said. "I knew I'd see you again."

"How?"

"When we said goodbye at the airport I knew I'd love you the rest of my life..."

"Oh, Uri."

"...and I had the sense you loved me, too."

"I did," I said, squeezing his hand. "And I do. More than anything. It was so hard getting on that plane."

Uri seemed to ignore my statement, caught up in his own emotions. "I had convinced myself that day that we were meant to be together. And I vowed to make it happen."

"It has happened. And we're happy, right? Let's just be happy."

Uri continued to be caught up in his own emotions.

"I told myself that once we were together I'd never let anything happen to you. I battled in my mind whether I should invite you to Rome. I knew it had the potential to blow up in my face. But I thought it would make a great book...and I had to see you again...I thought it would be different this time..."

"Uri," I said, shaking his hand to jolt him from his waking dream.

"I didn't think anything would happen. I thought I'd put the past behind me. I thought everyone had forgotten..."

"Uri," I said again,

"And now I've failed you..."

"Uri!" I yelled, and the restaurant seemed to go quiet.

Uri looked up from the table, into my eyes, and then glanced around the restaurant as if just awoken from a trance.

"I...I need a moment," he announced, jolting up from the table.

He quickly turned and made his way towards the back of the restaurant and disappeared into the men's room.

As he did, a piece of paper fell out of his blazer pocket.

CHAPTER TWENTY-FIVE

P rofessor Nevon,
Don't be foolish. You must know we are watching you and the girl. Don't question our authority or test our ability to do what is necessary to protect the truth.

The Custodian

It was no ordinary paper. It was a piece of thick parchment, folded in half three times. In the center on one side was a raised, red seal, an indicia containing a Latin phrase I couldn't translate. It looked official...

Other than the indicia, there were no markings on the outside of the note. No mailing address, no stamp, no inscription. Which means it had been delivered to Uri.

I wondered where he'd been when he'd received it. While he was with me in Rome? Or during his trip back to Jerusalem?

I hadn't intended to read it. I didn't *want* to read it. It was Uri's personal property. Invading his privacy was wrong, I knew, but I also felt that had he meant it to remain private, he wouldn't be carrying it around in his pocket.

Perhaps he'd meant to share it with me tonight. Perhaps it would bring me closer to the truth, reveal something that Uri couldn't—or wouldn't—reveal to me himself. Either way, I wasn't about to wait this time. This note, and its meaning, needed to be revealed. Our very lives could depend on it. So that's how I justified the betrayal. I would ask for forgiveness later.

Uri made his way back to the table with an apology as he sat down.

I smiled wanly at his apology. "Who's the Custodian?" I said.

Uri seemed to freeze and stop breathing for a moment. Finally, he shifted and said, "What?"

I pulled the note out from under the table and slid it across the table to him. "The Custodian, Uri. Who is he?"

"Where did you get that?"

"If fell out of your blazer pocket when you got up from the booth."

"I meant to tell you everything…"

"Tonight?"

Uri remained silent, and with that I knew the answer to my question.

"Then when?" I asked, agitated. "When would the time be right for you to tell me about something that involves me?"

"Be fair, Mara," he said. "There is more going on than you know. There is possible danger for us…"

"Then all the more reason for me to know!"

"I didn't want to frighten you, or implant thoughts of abandoning our mission."

"So you'd rather me be ignorant?"

"You are right," Uri said, taking my hand for the first time all evening. "I should have told you. I'm sorry."

I sighed. "Who's following us?"

"Benjamin."

"Of course it's Ben," I whispered under my breath, surprised and yet not that he'd been following us. He'd tailed us in Jerusalem to make sure we stayed out of trouble, but then wound up helping us gain access to the Talpiot Tomb when no one else would. I'd always been conflicted about Benjamin. There was a part of me that viewed him as an unrighteous bully, and another part of me that thought him a sympathetic hero.

"Is he the Custodian?"

Uri suppressed a laugh. "Doesn't he wish…"

"Who does Ben answer to?"

Uri wordlessly pointed to the note.

Then it hit me. The day Uri and I visited the ossuary shards in Jerusalem, Ben excused himself to take a cell phone call. What little of the conversation I heard seemed to be of a powerless Ben taking orders from a higher-up. He'd might've been talking to the Custodian, whoever that person was.

"I should've known," I said, more to myself than to Uri. Then, addressing Uri directly I said, "Ben called me the other day to apologize for the way he treated us at the Church of the Flagellation in Jerusalem."

"Funny, he didn't call me to apologize," Uri half-joked. "Did you tell him anything?"

"Like what? My pant size?" It was my turn to joke.

Uri laughed. "Did you tell him where you are staying...the specifics of our mission...Giovanni's involvement...?"

"I said as little as possible because I don't trust him."

"Good."

"He claims he knows what our ultimate goal is, but I neither confirmed nor denied it. Surprisingly he didn't push for details."

"Okay, anything else?" Uri asked.

"He knows we're a couple."

Uri's eyes widened at first, then softened as if he was OK with that truth being known. "How does he know that?"

"Body language, he said. And the way we look at each other and act around each other."

"Is it that obvious?"

I chuckled. "I guess so. Even Giovanni picked up on it."

"Is that what you two were whispering about the other night at the Basilica?"

"Yes."

"Well, it makes sense. Both men have known me a long time."

"In any case, Ben wished us luck."

"I guess that was a nice gesture, coming from someone like Ben."

"Yes, but it felt like more of a warning than a congratulations."

Uri furrowed his brows. "Oh..."

"Why he mean it that way?"

"I think he still views me as the enemy, a threat to his existence as peace-keeper and man of the law."

"*You're* a threat? He's the one following *us*."

Uri nodded as if acknowledging my concern and then said, "What else did you discuss?"

"He and Ziva are trying to have a baby."

"Yes, I knew that. Ziva told me."

"Does she know about us?"

"She's known about us longer than *we've* known about us..."

"Oh," was all I could say. Perhaps I had underestimated Ziva. I wanted to hate her because she'd broken Uri's heart. But in the end I had to believe she did what she thought was best for each of them as people. She had to allow Uri to be Uri, set him free, let him follow his passion without guilt. And she wanted to be able to move on with her own life, too, find peace in the fact that she wasn't holding someone back from their dream. And the only way to do that was with a clean break.

Similarly, I had to believe that's what was going on between Ben and Uri. Ben wanted to hate Uri for breaking Ziva's heart, for putting his passion for the Talpiot Tomb before his passion for Ziva, and for not loving her the way Ben knew he could. And no doubt there was some macho "I'm a better man than you'll ever be" bullshit thrown in the mix too.

Which is all well and good. I get that. Thomas and I had gone through a similar situation. We started our marriage off on the same page, wanting the same things, but as time went on, we changed. We became different people with different wants and needs. It's devastating when it happens, and you try to unite the person you were with the new person you want to be in order to keep your partner happy, but that really only sustains you for so long. That charade can be even more devastating than the reality of the situation.

I felt I understood the dynamics of the love triangle that had once existed between Uri, Ben and Ziva, so I chose not to dwell on it for too long. Mostly because there were more important things going on at the moment—namely, a feeling about Ben that didn't sit well with me. And all fingers were currently pointing to the mysterious figure lording over Ben like a puppeteer.

"Who's the Custodian?" I asked again.

Just then the waiter came over and placed two glasses of red wine on the table.

Uri looked up at the waiter in confusion. "We didn't order these," he said.

"Compliments of the man at the bar," the waiter said.

We both turned to look at the bar and saw a lone man sitting on a stool, watching us. He looked about middle-aged, with dark skin and white hair. He wore a suit and tie and the jacket was unbuttoned in such a way as to reveal the edge of a holstered gun clipped to his belt. I hadn't noticed him when we entered the restaurant, and judging from the look on Uri's face, neither had he.

The man raised a glass of what looked like beer and nodded at us.

"No," Uri whispered, lowering his head.

"Who is he?" I asked.

Uri calmly reached into his back pocket and pulled out his wallet. "We're leaving," he said, putting a hundred Euro note on the table. I doubt at the moment Uri cared about the change he wouldn't be getting.

I was too dumbfounded to speak.

"On the count of three we're both going to casually get up and make our way towards the restrooms," Uri instructed. "There's a door at the end of that hallway. We're going to exit through that doorway. Do you understand?"

"Who is he, Uri?"

Uri's face was stern. "Do you understand?"

"No. I don't."

"We have to go. *Now*."

"You're scaring me."

"On the count of three, okay?"

I nodded.

"One."

I grabbed my purse and secured it around my shoulder. My body trembled.

"Two."

Uri slid out of the booth, stood, and reached out for my hand. I shifted my way out of the booth and took his hand to steady my wobbly legs.

Uri smiled.

"Three."

CHAPTER TWENTY-SIX

I was pacing in my hotel room, deep in thought.

What was happening? One minute Uri and I were having a nice dinner, albeit punctuated by an intense conversation about our fate in Rome. The next minute we were being stalked by an unknown man with a hidden agenda and a gun on his hip.

Uri had made us flee the restaurant and hop into a cab to avoid being tailed. From there we rushed up to my hotel room where Uri left me, alone.

Lock the door, he'd said.

Stay here.

Don't leave until I come get you.

He'd said he'd be back, but he didn't say when. Of course he hadn't said when. I fired questions at him, all of them unanswered.

What was happening? I continued asking myself, still pacing. I had to know once and for all. Uri had to tell me before—

BANG! BANG BANG!

The pounding on the door startled me and I froze.

Maybe it was Uri. No, Uri would've announced himself. And he had just left....

I peeked through the peephole hoping to see Uri. Instead there were three men in black suits: the man from the restaurant flanked by two younger, more muscular men.

"Miss Beltane!" the older gentleman said. He had a thick, Italian accent.

One of the younger men reached up to the door with a big fist.

BANG! BANG! BANG!

Should I speak to them? Maybe if I stayed silent they'd think I wasn't here and they'd go away.

"Miss Beltane!" the older gentleman said again. "We know you're in there... We just want to talk..."

126

At first I thought silence was the best answer. If I didn't open the door or speak to them how would they even know I was here? And if they thought I was here, what would they do? Bust the door down? And then what? Rough me up? Kidnap me?

On the flip side, if I spoke to them, maybe even let them in, maybe I'd finally get some answers. Answers that Uri seemed reluctant to give.

I stepped up to the door and looked through the peephole again. The three men still stood there. The older gentleman looked at his watch.

Stay here.

Don't talk to anyone.

Don't open the door for anyone. Not even hotel staff.

Uri's instructions bounced around in my brain. Did he know someone would come looking for us here? If so, why leave me alone?

My brain still teetered on the edge of remaining silent and letting the enemy in. What should I do? But then the older gentleman said something that made up my mind.

"We have Uri...."

I was instantly scared—and very pissed off.

"Who are you?" I said. "What do you want?"

"Open the door, Miss Beltane," the older gentleman said. "We just want to talk."

"I don't trust you."

"I understand." There was a pause.

"Is Uri okay?" I asked.

"Open the door and I'll tell you."

"If you want to talk it'll have to be under my rules."

"Which are?"

"I'll talk, but you're not coming in. We'll talk through the closed door."

I checked to make sure the door was locked and the deadbolt engaged.

The older man chuckled. "Try to be reasonable, Miss Beltane."

"That is being reasonable. I'll tell you whatever you want to know, as long as you stay out there. Seems fair enough to me."

"So be it. Let's talk."

"First thing's first. Is Uri okay?"

"Uri is fine, but I can't say for how long."

"What the hell does that mean?"

"What that means is the longer it takes you to tell me what I want to know, the closer Uri gets to *not* being okay."

"Who the hell are you?" I yelled.

"The longer we play these games, Miss Beltane, the less time Uri has."

"Until what?"

"Open the door and I'll tell you."

"If I open this door you have to promise that Uri stays safe and unharmed."

There was a pause. I looked out the peephole just as the older gentleman leaned over and whispered something under his breath to the man on his right. The young man wordlessly nodded.

"I promise," the older man said, his head bowed.

I trusted Uri, believed that he was looking out for my safety when he told me to barricade myself inside my hotel room. There was a good reason why he wanted me to listen to him. And I really wanted to comply. But had I known at the time Uri would be in harm's way I never would've agreed to that. So while I didn't trust the three men on the other side of the door, I did what I felt I had to do: which was everything Uri told me *not* to do. After all, if Uri was in danger, I wouldn't be able to live with myself if something happened to him.

I disengaged the deadbolt and unlocked the door. I opened the door a crack and peeked through, eying each of the three men in turn.

The older gentleman smiled. "We meet at last..."

"Open the door!" the young man to his right hissed.

The older gentleman placed a hand on his shoulder.

"May we come in, Miss Beltane?" the older man said.

I opened the door and the men casually entered single file. The older gentleman faced me, keeping his eyes on me, smiling. He stood several feet in front of me, along with one of his younger henchman. The other young man, the one who insisted I open the door, stood back, scanning the room as if looking for something.

I spoke first.

"Uri is safe, right? You promised."

The older gentleman sighed. "Ah, Miss Beltane. I'm afraid I never was good at keeping my promises."

And with that, the young man standing next to him grabbed me, forced a hood over my head, and I was instantly thrust into darkness.

CHAPTER TWENTY-SEVEN

I could only surmise I was being taken to see the Custodian.

The Order of Franciscans Minor is divided into Custodies, or geographic areas. Each Custody has one person who rules all the Franciscans within that custody.

And that person is the Custodian.

The Custodian we were dealing with was a man who'd sent Uri a disturbing warning note, and he was in charge of the Custody of the Holy Land. He oversaw the work of 300 friars and 100 sisters throughout Israel, the Palestinian territories, Jordan, Syria, Lebanon, Egypt, and the islands of Cyprus and Rhodes.

I already knew the Custodian oversaw not only people, but property—namely, the Church of the Holy Sepulchre, basilicas in Bethlehem and Nazareth, and the Church of the Flagellation.

What I didn't know was why the Custodian had been following Uri and me since Jerusalem. What secret were they keeping that they were afraid we'd reveal?

Most definitely it involved Saint Peter. Was he really buried in Jerusalem in a bone box that bore his name? Could we have been right all along? Is that the truth they were trying to protect at all costs? Hopefully I was about to find out.

I was trying to connect the dots, arm myself for when I got to my destination and came face to face with whoever had been taunting us. But suddenly, while being walked from my hotel room to a car with a hood over my head, I felt my head get heavy and my brain go numb, as waves of unconsciousness blurred my vision until finally I blacked out.

When I awoke I was in a dark room, tied to a chair. I blinked my eyes to adjust to my surroundings. The older gentleman stood off to my left; to my right was an empty chair. Directly in front of me a man was similarly tied to a chair. His head bobbed slightly up and down as if fighting consciousness and as he moaned I realized who it was.

Uri.

My head was still fuzzy from whatever chemical I had been drugged with. I took several deep breaths to allow more oxygen into my lungs and shook my head to clear my thoughts.

"Uri!" I called. "Wake up! Open your eyes and look at me!"

Uri looked up at me, his eyes heavily hooded, and blinked several times.

The older gentleman approached me. As he did I yelled at him, "What did you do to him?"

"Nothing severe," a familiar voice said from the shadows.

As Ben emerged from the back corner of the room I struggled against the ties that bound me to the chair. I could feel the plastic ties digging into the flesh of my wrists. If I could break free I would punch Benjamin Schwarz square in the face.

"Ben!" I spit his name out. "I should've known you were involved!"

"Now, now, Mara," he said, approaching me and standing next to the older gentleman. "Fighting will only make it worse."

"I swear to God if either one of you hurt him..." I said, looking at each of them, continuing to struggle.

Ben walked back to where Uri sat and lifted his head. "Look here, Mara. We didn't touch a hair on his head. Not even a scratch, see?" Ben ran his fingers across both sides of Uri's face and Uri moaned.

"You drugged us!" I said.

Ben rejoined the older gentleman, who continued to look down at me, smiling. "Uri wouldn't go willingly," Ben said. "And my friend here sensed *you* wouldn't either."

The other gentleman finally spoke. "Simply a precaution, I assure you. You are returning to normal and so is Uri. He is otherwise unharmed. Just as I promised..."

I looked over at Uri, whose head was fully upright. He was looking at me and groggily shaking his head, as if willing me to remain silent.

I looked up at the older gentleman. "Who are you?"

"Let me introduce you to my friend and colleague Antonio Lupoli," Ben said. "Inspector General of the Corps of Gendarmerie."

"Commanding officer of the police and security force of Vatican City, at your service," Antonio said, bowing slightly in a mocking fashion.

"You're just a cop?" I said, half-mockingly. I felt fully alert now, the effects of the drug having finally worn off.

The smile melted from Antonio's face. "I am responsible for the security and order of the entire Vatican City State," he snarled. "Including the safety of the Pope."

"Good for you," I said. "What do you want with us?"

"Public order. Police matters. Criminal investigations," Antonio said. "It all falls on my shoulders. And what you and Uri did was a breach of Vatican City security."

"I don't know what you think we did, Officer Lupoli," I said, "but I assure you we did nothing wrong. In fact, you don't even know why Uri and I are in Rome. You have no evidence to prove anything, so why don't you let us go?"

Suddenly Uri shifted in his chair, wincing as the ties dug into his hands. He spoke but it was too soft for any of us to hear. Ben took a few steps and leaned over Uri. "What was that, Uri?" he asked.

"Say nothing more, Mara," Uri said, looking straight at me and ignoring Ben.

I should've been scared out of my mind. Here I was in a strange country, tied to a chair, surrounded by armed cops and Vatican officials who were treating me like a criminal, swearing that I'd broken the law. They stood over me menacingly and were assumingly using Uri as bait in order to get me to talk. It was a scene straight out of a crime thriller, one that ended with the heroine either escaping with her life or falling dead in the street.

But somehow I wasn't scared at all. In fact, I felt empowered.

"What are we doing here, fellas?" I asked. "What do you want?"

"We want information," Ben said.

"There's nothing to tell," Uri said.

"Hear that?" I said. "There's nothing to tell. We don't know anything!"

Suddenly Antonio was in my face. "What do you know about the truth of Saint Peter?"

I flinched at his abrupt closeness. Out of the corner of my eye I saw Uri lurch forward in his chair, struggling against the plastic strips that tied his wrists to the chair.

So there *was* some hidden secret about Saint Peter that someone wanted to stay hidden. Antonio had pretty much just admitted it. Was it the Franciscans who held the secret? Had the Pope entrusted it to them? If so, why was Ben here?

"Leave her alone!" Uri yelled.

Antonio turned his attention to Uri, walking closer to his chair. "Answer my question and I will leave both of you alone..."

"We know nothing," I answered for Uri. "Whatever secret you're keeping, we have no idea what it is."

"And Giovanni?" Ben said, walking over to a door I hadn't seen until just now. "Does he know nothing as well?"

"Professor Carlo?" I said. "He has nothing to do with this!"

"Ah, but he does..." Ben said. He banged hard three times on the wooden door. The door opened and the professor staggered inside, led by another young man in a black suit. The professor's clothes were dirtied, his face haggard, his steps labored. He looked older than his sixty plus years. He looked around the room in confusion. When his eyes connected on Uri and then me they widened in disbelief. His knees buckled and he cried out, "Per favore, lasciate andare!"

Please, let them go!

"Giovanni, are you hurt?" I asked, but he seemed to not hear me, like he was in shock.

Ben grabbed him by the arm and led him past me and Uri to the third chair to my right. As Giovanni walked by he looked at Uri and me each in turn and apologized in broken Italian, choking on his words.

"Are you okay?" Uri asked Giovanni, and again he seemed lost in his own thoughts.

Giovanni was forced to sit but was not bound to the chair as we had been. He continued to whimper softly but then, as if his fright had been taken over by anger he looked up at Antonio. "Why, brother? Tell me why...?"

"Brother?" I said, looking at Giovanni and then over to Uri. Uri's shoulders shrank and he bowed his head and it was at that moment I knew I'd stumbled upon one of the secrets he had been keeping from me.

Giovanni's connections.

"Well, well, well," Ben said, standing in the middle of the circle our three chairs created. "Isn't this a fancy reunion?" He looked at Uri and Giovanni and then, with what seemed to be his most evil snarl, he said to me, "Now, tell us what you know..."

CHAPTER TWENTY-EIGHT

B en and Officer Lupoli stood to my left, keeping an eye on the three of us. Uri and I were still zip-tied to our chairs, and Giovanni, perhaps not perceived as a threat, was not. Nothing prevented him from taking action, if he so wished.

Nothing except Officer Lupoli's sidearm.

Even if Giovanni had run for help, where would he go? The Vatican City police had kidnapped an innocent American tourist, her Israeli boyfriend, and a Roman citizen, and were holding them captive who-knows-where for reasons known only to them. They'd get away with it because one of the men holding us captive was the head of security for the entire city state.

The Roman police? They would probably laugh in Giovanni's face and say it wasn't their problem.

The three of us were on our own.

"I kept my promise," Officer Lupoli said to me. "Now it's time for you to keep yours. Tell us what you know..."

"How do you and Ben know each other?" I said, ignoring his command in an attempt to buy us some time.

"What does it matter?" he said. "Answer us!"

"It doesn't matter," I said. Out of the corner of my eye I could see Uri furiously shaking his head at me. I chose to ignore him, too. "I'm just curious."

Ben sighed and whispered to Officer Lupoli, who nodded.

"Antonio and I go way back," Ben said, starting to pace the room. "We were both once part of Pope John Paul II's security detail. We were plain-clothes officers who worked directly for the Pope through the Vatican. Our job was to protect the Pope at all times. Kind of like your Secret Service."

"That's how you met?" I asked.

Ben now stood directly behind Uri. "Yes."

"We became good friends and honed our skills as security agents over several years," Officer Lupoli said.

"Then what?" I asked, looking over at Giovanni, who was alertly watching the scene before him but choosing to remain silent.

"Then an officer position became available within the Jerusalem police," Ben explained. "I welcomed the idea of protecting my country. Eventually I worked my way up to chief of police."

"And you?" I motioned to Officer Lupoli.

"Soon after Ben left, the position as head of security for Vatican City became vacant," Officer Lupoli said. "I interviewed and got the job."

"And you've been torturing innocent tourists and your own family members ever since..." I said.

Officer Lupoli clenched his fists and ran towards me, his face a mask of anger. "Watch yourself, young lady!" he hissed. I could feel his hot breath on my face he was so close. "Remember who kept his word and didn't hurt your boyfriend."

"Leave her alone!" Uri cried out. He was struggling to free his hands as Ben hovered behind his chair, almost menacingly.

I eyed the officer, swallowed my pride and said, "Thank you for keeping your word."

He smiled and shrunk away a few steps as if satisfied with my statement. Ben, on the other hand, didn't look so satisfied. In fact, he seemed is if he was losing patience. He shuffled from side to side, sighed several times, looked at his watch twice.

I gave Uri a nod and glance of encouragement, letting him know that I was okay and had everything under control.

"Got somewhere to be, Ben?" I asked.

"You're stalling, Miss Beltane," he said. "You know it and I know it. We've been more than patient with you. Gave you everything you asked for. Now it's time for you keep your end of the bargain."

I paused a moment before answering, weighing my options.

"Just one more question," I said.

"No more questions!" Officer Lupoli yelled, his anger renewed. He approached me again, his hand outstretched as if about to strike my face.

Just then Giovanni jumped from his chair and lunged at his brother. I twisted to the side and winced, bracing to be hit by a flailing arm, a bumped elbow, a misplaced fist. Giovanni managed to push Officer Lupoli away from me, but received a blow to the stomach for his efforts.

He grunted, recovered from the gut punch and went after his brother again. "I should have kicked your ass a long time ago!" Giovanni yelled.

"Just remember everything I've done for you!" Officer Lupoli said, responding with another blow to his brother's stomach. "And don't forget it was me that got your friends into the basilica that night!"

"That's enough!" Ben said through the cacophony of yelling and grunts. But no one was paying attention to him.

Giovanni positioned himself to charge Officer Lupoli again. "And then you tailed them and kidnapped them! For what?"

"Enough!" Ben yelled again, and again it fell on deaf ears.

Officer Lupoli put his arms out to block the attack. "You lied to me, brother! You knew what they were up to, knew the consequences of their snooping. You know it's my job to protect Vatican City at all costs!"

"ENOUGH!" Ben's voice bellowed through the chamber, commanding to be heard.

The roar was enough to stop the brothers in their tracks. I looked over at Ben who stood hunched over Uri, a Swiss Army knife to his throat.

"Enough," he said one final time.

Uri's eyes were large and unblinking. With one quick flick of the wrist Ben could end his life...and mine. The thought of it sent me over the edge.

"No, don't!" I yelled, my heart suddenly pounding.

"I have told you what you want to know," Ben said, pulling the knife closer to Uri's throat, the blade now skimming his skin. "Now it's your turn to talk."

CHAPTER TWENTY-NINE

I had to do something.

Quick.

"Don't do this, Ben!" I pleaded. "Think of Ziva. Think of the baby!"

Ben's shoulders tensed and he pushed the knife blade further into Uri's throat. One more millimeter and he'd break the skin.

Uri's eyes widened even further. Other than that, he remained utterly still and silent. Exactly what I needed him to do.

"What are you talking about?" Ben said.

"Ziva's pregnant," I said.

Stay still, Uri, I pleaded with my eyes.

No sudden movements.

Let me handle this.

The knife was still perched at Uri's throat. I had to believe that at any moment Ben would strike. I couldn't allow that to happen.

"How would you know?" Ben said, his hand starting to tremble.

"Because she told me, you fool!" I hissed.

With that, Ben pulled the knife from Uri's throat, rushed around his chair and charged at me, the knife now pointing directly at my chest.

CHAPTER THIRTY

B en charged at me with the knife. The moment of impact seemed to take forever, replaying in slow motion in my mind every time I recalled it. Later I realized that the whole event played out in only several seconds.

Ben lunged forward, a look of determination on his face. I remember hearing Uri yell out in anguish. I remember seeing Giovanni's terrified face. And I remember Ben rushing me from the side, his chest slamming into my left shoulder, nearly knocking me over, the knife deflected down, the snap of the plastic ties being cut behind my back, the twinge of pain as my hands were finally released.

Mostly I remember feeling relief.

Not because Ben hadn't injured any of us. But because I'd been right about Ben. Physical harm was never an option in his mind.

Ben was an angry man. But he wasn't a killer.

I knew that from the time I spent with him in Jerusalem. Sure, he'd followed me through the streets of Jerusalem, had me arrested and thrown in jail. But all those actions were justified. Uri and I had broken the law, and Ben was only doing his job. He'd never once gotten violent, pulled his gun on us, laid a hand on either of us.

Benjamin Schwarz played the role of tough guy because he felt he had to. His job required it. His men expected it.

And his wife, Ziva, learned to accept it.

At the end of a shift, he had a hard time letting the tough guy go. When he found out about the baby, he knew he'd have to change that. He wondered if he'd be able to.

He worried he wouldn't be a good enough father.

He stressed about having another mouth to feed.

He hoped he'd make his kid proud of him.

Ziva listened to all his fears, all his anxieties, and did what she could to assuage them.

She could see the stress starting to build, though. The stress of a new baby combined with the stress of his job. Add to that a new job he'd recently taken on.

He was working on the side on a high-profile case. He was recruited by some very powerful people and it required occasional travel to Rome. That was all Ben could tell Ziva. He was sworn to secrecy.

She knew her colleague Uri Nevon was in Rome at the time. She wondered if the case Ben was on involved him. She worried her husband might implode from pressure at any moment, and she worried Uri might be in trouble again.

That made her think of me.

She wondered if I had something to do with it. If I knew what was going on.

I knew all this because she called me asking for help.

"On your feet! Now!" Ben barked at me.

I rose on wobbly legs and massaged my throbbing arms.

He cut Uri loose next, folded up the small knife, and returned it to his back pocket.

"You, too!" he ordered Uri.

Uri stood and rushed over to me, grabbing me tightly.

"Are you okay?" he whispered.

"I am now," I said.

"Okay, love birds," Ben said. "Let's go! You too, Professor Maderno."

One of Officer Lupoli's men opened the door and stood guard beside it.

Officer Lupoli pushed a finger into Giovanni's back and told him to get walking. Ben motioned for Uri and me to follow.

"Where are you taking us?" I asked.

"If I can't make you talk, maybe the Custodian will."

CHAPTER THIRTY-ONE

"Where are we?" I whispered.

Uri sat to my right and Giovanni to my left on one side of a large rectangular table. The chairs on the other side of the table were empty.

We were supposedly waiting for the Custodian.

"Not sure," Giovanni whispered back.

"Silence!" Office Lupoli said. He stood motionless in front of the door we'd come through a few moments before. He eyed the three of us like a hawk.

Ben was on the opposite side of the room, quietly pacing the floor. Something about the Custodian rattled him, unnerved him. He never seemed like himself whenever the subject of the Custodian came up. He seemed to flinch at the very mention of his name.

I remembered the time at the Church of the Flagellation in Jerusalem when Ben was taking orders from someone over the phone. He was pacing then, too, running his fingers through his hair. Some time later I imagined it was the Custodian on the other end of the line. Now I was sure of it.

It was hard for me to imagine that someone as intimidating at Benjamin Schwarz could himself be intimidated.

"We're inside the Palace of the Governorate," Giovanni said softly. "The capital building of the Vatican."

"Sounds familiar," I whispered. "Where's that?"

"Directly behind Saint Peter's Basilica."

We had walked for what felt like forever, down corridors, up numerous flights of stairs, until we arrived at this room. We had been inside the whole time. I got the sense an elaborate tunnel system connected all the buildings inside the Vatican complex.

"Consider yourself a VIP," Officer Lupoli said loudly, as if to indicate he heard our exchange. "Only employees of the Vatican City are allowed inside this building."

I looked around the room, at the deep rich colors of dark wood on the walls, floor and ceiling. Gold and bronze statuettes lined the mantelpiece above the marble fireplace. Ornate paintings hung on the wall, dozens of them, mostly Renaissance masters, probably all priceless.

"He can't hold us much longer," Giovanni said to me, loudly enough for his brother to hear. "He knows we've done nothing wrong."

"Brother!" Officer Lupoli yelled, and we both jumped, startled.

"What do you mean?" I asked Giovanni, who only smirked and motioned to his brother. I redirected the question to Officer Lupoli. "So we're not going to jail?"

"Vatican City has no prison system," he said condescendingly, as if I ought to know that fact. "So I couldn't throw you in jail even if I wanted to." Then, looking me dead in the eye he added, "But I could hand you over to the Italian authorities."

"Why don't you?" I said.

"I'd have to get permission from the Holy See first in order to have you punished. But as you can imagine, the Pope is very busy and I don't see the need to waste his time. He has much bigger issues to contend with."

"But you said earlier that what we'd done was considered a breach of Vatican City security."

"A breach of security has been committed..." Officer Lupoli said. "But no actual *crime* has been committed." His nostrils flared now, as if he hated admitting the limitations of his position.

Just then Ben cleared his throat. "Stop!" he said firmly. "Antonio, you've said quite enough. And you," he added, pointing at me, "enough questions."

"So if you can't throw us in a jail for a crime we didn't commit, then what is this all about?" I asked in defiance of Ben's insistence we keep quiet.

"It is out of my hands now, Miss Beltane," Ben said shrugging. "I did what I was asked to do. The rest is up to the discretion of the Custodian."

"The Custodian, the Custodian, the Custodian..." I said, sighing. "I keep hearing his name but he's like a ghost. I'm beginning to think he's a figment of your imagination."

Just then the door opened and a bearded, robed man entered. Office Lupoli stepped out his way.

"I assure you I am very real," the man announced, his voice meek yet self-assured.

Finally, after weeks of speculation and rumor and mystery, I would finally get to meet the person I'd heard so much about, a man revered and simultaneously feared.

The Custodian.

CHAPTER THIRTY-TWO

T he Custodian seemed to float over to the table. "Miss Mara
Beltane," he said, seeming to ignore the others in the room. We
locked eyes and I stood to greet him properly. Uri and Giovanni stood
as well, but the Custodian hardly noticed; he kept his blue-eyed gaze
on me.

He held out his hand. "My name is Roberto Agnelli. I am the
Custodian of the Holy Land."

His smile was warm and friendly. His voice was soothing. His
handshake, soft and inviting. His attire and his mannerisms screamed
piety and his long, grayish hair and beard hinted at years of hard labor
and sacrifice. He wasn't much taller than me, but what he lacked in
stature he made up for in charm and self-assuredness.

What was it about this man that put Ben at unease? I was neither
intimidated nor uneasy. Instead I felt...comfortable. Like I was about
ready to have a cup of tea with my grandfather.

"It's nice to finally meet you," I said.

"The pleasure is truly all mine," he said, clasping his hands together
in front on him. Then, motioning to the table he said, "Please, sit."

Suddenly Ben rushed toward the table. "Roberto, I must insist—"

The Custodian held up two fingers on his right hand and Ben
was instantly silenced. "Benjamin, my dear boy..." was all he said. Ben
shrank back and resumed pacing the floor.

The Custodian then turned his attention to Uri, who stood a few
paces to my right. "I'm a big fan on your work, Professor Nevon.
Especially the peer-reviewed work you published several years ago
about Mary Magdalene. Very well done."

Uri bowed slightly. "That's an honor coming from you, Sir."

"Please, call me Roberto." Then, looking around the room to each
of the men in turn, Roberto said, "Gentleman, if you wouldn't mind,
I'd like a moment alone with Miss Beltane."

CHAPTER THIRTY-THREE

"**I** don't wish to waste your time," Roberto said, "So I'll get right down to it."

The Custodian and I were sitting next to each other at the table. He sat back in his chair, legs crossed, and I sat on the edge of mine.

"Please, call me Mara."

"You've caused some trouble, Mara." His voice seemed to have lost some of its friendliness; it was now tinged with irritation.

"Honestly, I don't know what I did wrong. I'm just a writer in search of a story."

Roberto thought about my comment a moment, stroked his beard, cleared his throat. "Did you find what you were looking for?"

"Ben and Officer Lupoli seem to think so. Why else kidnap the three of us and interrogate and torture us?"

"Because I hired them to." He said it so nonchalantly that I scarce believed he said it.

"You—you what?"

Roberto gently grasped my arm. "Let me rephrase myself."

"Good idea," I said, laughing nervously.

"As the Custodian of the Holy Land my primary function is the protection of ancient relics and treasures within my jurisdiction. While that doesn't include the Talpiot tomb—which you successfully...*navigated*...two years ago—it does include the Church of the Flagellation, which you most recently insisted is housing the remains of Saint Peter."

"The Israel Antiquities Authority is in control of the Talpiot tomb. That's why you didn't come after me two years ago," I said, more to myself than to Roberto.

"Among other reasons."

"Which are?"

"First, I thought you were simply the next in a long line of bible hunters out to solve an unsolvable mystery."

"You don't think the provenance of the Talpiot tomb will ever be discovered?"

"I don't." He paused, then continued. "Secondly, I thought with the publication of your Talpiot tomb novel, you'd simply move on. I very much enjoyed the book, by the way."

"Thank you," I said, then added quickly, "move on to what?"

Roberto crossed his arms. "Oh, I don't know. The next fiction fad. Vampires, werewolves, the Apocalypse..."

"I'm not interested in the next big thing."

"I soon realized that after I'd heard you were in Rome."

"How'd you find out?"

Roberto simply shrugged and smiled and I realized he would not tell me.

I searched the Franciscan's eyes. They were still warm and friendly. Although he was clearly upset, I felt that he wasn't here to harm me. And I already knew he couldn't arrest me or throw me in jail. So I really had nothing to fear.

"Fair enough," I said. "So if you weren't worried about me digging around the Talpiot tomb, why are you now worried about my presence in Rome and Vatican City? I mean, if you have nothing to hide..."

Roberto leaned in and whispered, "Maybe I do have something to hide."

"So you hired two cops to kidnap me?"

"Not kidnap you," the Franciscan said. "Monitor you."

"Why Ben and Antonio?"

"Because you and Uri have history with Benjamin. I knew he'd be able to figure out what you were thinking, where you'd go next. And I chose Antonio because he knows Vatican City better than anyone. And he has the power to enforce its rules."

"Rome isn't even within your jurisdiction. You rule over Jerusalem and other areas of the Holy Land. Technically, you have no right to be doing any of this."

"We all answer to someone. Isn't that right, Mara?"

"Yes," I said cautiously. "Where are you going with this?"

"I don't have jurisdiction here. But my employer does."

"Your employer?"

"Perhaps that's not the right word. Let's just say I answer to a higher authority that is nervous about your presence in Rome."

"You mean the Pope?"

Roberto nodded. "I am an officer of the Franciscan order. My appointment was approved by the Pope and the Holy See. Therefore, I answer to them."

"The Pope knows who I am?" I asked, flabbergasted.

The Custodian nodded and answered simply, "Yes."

"Why did he choose you to track me?"

"The Holy See has neither the time nor the resources to dedicate to this special, short-term mission. They needed someone with knowledge of both Jerusalem and Rome, and who would hold the other people involved accountable for their actions."

"You mean the cops who drugged us, kidnapped us, and nearly threatened us with our lives?"

Roberto bowed his head, as if ashamed. Then he looked me in the eye with what I believed to be utmost sincerity. "I am truly sorry for their actions. I did not wish for them to take such extreme measures."

How was I to respond to that? Take my anger out on a devoted man of God? Threaten to sue the Vatican?

"I take full responsibility for what Benjamin and Antonio did to the three of you," Roberto continued. "If there's anything I can do to make up for your suffering please let me know."

"How about you let us go and we forget all about this?" I said.

The Custodian smirked and I sensed that wasn't an option.

"We're not criminals," I said. "You can't hold us here. We didn't do anything wrong..."

Roberto continued to look at me, expressionless. As a Christian wasn't he supposed to feel empathy? Wasn't his religion based on forgiveness and compassion? Forgive others of their trespasses and all that? Finally, he spoke.

"There might have been an accusation that my Custody was intentionally hiding evidence of Saint Peter's burial in Jerusalem..."

"You're concerned about that? I'm a nobody! Who's going to listen to me?"

"You do intend to write a book about it..."

"A novel!" I said, perhaps too harshly. But Roberto maintained his composure, nonplussed by my sudden outburst. I took a deep breath. "Roberto, I write fiction for a living. Which means I make stuff up and mix it with some truths."

Yes, I'd made some accusations about the Custody of the Holy Land intentionally hiding evidence of Saint Peter's burial in Jerusalem, namely a bone box with his name on it. And with Giovanni's help Uri and I had gained access to areas of Saint Peter's Basilica that we had no right being in, places that are off-limits to the public. You could make an argument—albeit a weak one—that we broke into one of the most revered places in all of Christendom.

But a 'special mission' of cops to spy on us, watch our every move, kidnap us, torture us, threaten us? The punishment didn't fit the crime. And what Ben and Officer Lupoli did to us was certainly crossing the line.

The more I thought about it, the angrier I got. Uri and I weren't mercenaries sent in to infiltrate and take down the Catholic Church. I was nothing more than a writer researching her next book. I had nothing to hide. No vendettas. No acts of revenge to exact. I wasn't a threat to anyone.

And they were acting like I had discovered evidence of a two-thousand year-old cover-up, some secret that had the power to upend everything we thought we knew about—

Suddenly an idea hit me.

It was a radical one, and would probably never fly.

But I had to try.

If I thought there was any other way out of the mess I found myself in, I would've tried it.

And the Custodian *did* ask.

CHAPTER THIRTY-FOUR

"So you said the Pope is nervous about my presence in Rome and the Vatican..."

I was pacing the floor now, thinking out loud, hatching a cockamamie plan to have my cake and eat it, too.

The Custodian nodded, watching me closely.

"I can't understand why, unless he thinks I've stumbled across some controversial information that would turn his religion on its head."

Roberto remained silent.

"I explained earlier that I'm simply a writer looking for a story. But perhaps I haven't been totally honest with you..."

At that, the Custodian leaned forward in his chair.

"Perhaps Uri and I found something. Something that would prove Saint Peter truly was buried in Jerusalem." I stopped pacing and looked at Roberto. "How would that make you feel?"

"Knowledge like that has the power to affect billions of believers around the world. I'd fear the information might get into the wrong hands."

"That is why you're here in Rome, right? To stop me from finding and releasing such information?"

Roberto nodded again.

"Do you think I already possess this information?"

The Custodian rose from his chair and approached me. "I received orders and I carried them out. Now here we are."

"C'mon, Roberto. You must have an opinion. You must think I have something or why else come here yourself? Why the private meeting? Why are we here?"

Roberto stroked his beard and sighed heavily. I took that opportunity to strike.

"I won't stop," I said. "If I have the information, I will release it to the world. And if I don't, I'll keep searching until I've uncovered every rock for the answer."

The Custodian's eyes suddenly went cold. "Why must you resort to threats, Mara?"

I ignored his question. "You said if there was anything you could do to make up for my suffering, I should ask."

"Yes, and I meant it."

"Well then, here's what I propose."

And with that, I launched into my request.

CHAPTER THIRTY-FIVE

"**H**ave you lost your mind?" Uri said. Then he hugged me tight, kissed me on the cheek and said, "That's brilliant! Risky and crazy, but brilliant!"

Several moments before, I'd unleashed my crazy request on the Custodian of the Holy Land. It was foolish and impetuous, but I figured I had nothing to lose.

At best I'd be thrown out of the country. At worst I'd be turned over to the Italian authorities.

Turns out, neither of those things happened. After some quiet contemplation and some pacing of his own, Roberto considered my request and said he'd be in touch within the hour. Upon leaving my company, he said, "You drive a hard bargain, Miss Beltane. I hope to see you again soon. Best of luck with your next book. I'm sure it will also be a best-seller."

Now Uri and I were reunited. It was just the two of us in the room where the negotiations had begun. After Uri was ushered back into the room by one of Officer Lupoli's men, I immediately told him the details of my conversation with the Custodian.

"So now what?" Uri asked.

"We wait." Then, realizing Giovanni wasn't with Uri, I asked about him.

"They let him go," Uri said.

"They let him go, just like that?"

"He was right. They had nothing on him. They placed most of the blame on his brother, Antonio, because he's the one who gave Giovanni the keys."

"What will happen to Officer Lupoli?"

"Who knows? Perhaps nothing at all..."

"What were the brothers fighting about?"

"Their relationship is...complicated. Remind me to tell you about it sometime."

"Okay," I said, laughing. Then, more to myself than to Uri I said, "I hope I see Giovanni again..."

"You will," Uri said, smiling.

"Where did Ben scamper off to?"

Uri shrugged. "I thought you'd know. I haven't seen him."

"Probably back under the rock he crawled out from." I started pacing the floor, hoping the hour would pass by quickly. "So when did you figure out it was Ben who was following us?"

"I didn't know it was Ben at first. I became suspicious during my brief trip home to Jerusalem."

I stopped pacing and eyed Uri.

"In the days leading up to my flight I'd received several strange phone calls, too many to dismiss as coincidence," Uri explained. "It felt like the Talpiot tomb all over again."

"I wish you'd told me."

"I'm sorry. I didn't mean to keep it from you. I just didn't want to worry you if it turned out to be nothing."

He sighed and sat down at the table. "I did what I needed to do at Hebrew University and then decided to pay Ben a visit. I thought maybe he could shed some light on the situation. You know, in light of our...altercation...at the Church of the Flagellation."

"I'm sure that meeting went well," I joked, sitting down across the table from Uri.

"That's when I knew Ben was involved. Something about his demeanor, his sudden anger when I asked him simple questions. It made me really uneasy."

"Yeah, Ben sure has a way with people."

"He denied involvement in anything we were doing in Rome, saying it was out of his jurisdiction. Then he offered to keep his eyes open and warn me if he became aware of anything."

"He was throwing you off the trail, the trail that he himself was on."

"Right. And I wasn't taking any chances. I went to see Lev right away. Which was a mistake."

"Why?"

"Confronting Ben is what tipped him off. I should've known that Ben would then visit Lev and interrogate him. And then Lev would have to lie about his involvement."

"Don't hold yourself responsible," I said. "Ben would've interrogated Lev anyway. Besides, Lev was hardly involved so there was nothing for him to lie about."

Uri sighed. "True enough."

I suddenly remembered the frantic phone call I had gotten from Lev. He'd asked if I was okay, then asked me to promise not to tell Uri that he called me. I was more worried for Lev's safety at that point than I was for my own, given the loud voices in the background and the hushed and hurried tone of Lev's voice. Lev's last words to me that day were a warning: be careful, they might come for you.

I didn't know it then but I knew now that it was Ben who Lev had been referring to. Lev was worried Ben might come for me in Rome.

And Lev had been right. Ben did come for Uri and me.

If only I knew what he intended to do with us now.

CHAPTER THIRTY-SIX

I paced the floor again, this time for what seemed like hours. I looked at my watch. Forty-five minutes had passed since the Custodian had left.

Where was he? And where was Ben?

Tired of pacing, I collapsed into a chair next to Uri and sighed heavily.

Uri eyed me, a squinty-eyed look of suspicion.

"What?" I said.

"Ziva called you..."

"The day we went underneath Saint Peter's. Are you surprised?"

"Quite. She's strong and stubborn. She doesn't ask for help easily. She sees it as a sign of weakness."

"I sensed that. But I also sensed she was genuinely worried about Ben's mental state. She loves him, God help her."

Uri laughed, then eyed me again.

"What?"

"Ziva didn't tell me about the baby. You, apparently, are the only one who knew."

I smiled and squinted mischievously. "You think you're the only one with secrets?"

Just then the door opened and Ben emerged.

"Okay, love birds," he said, standing at the table in front of us.

Uri and I stood to face our fate.

CHAPTER THIRTY-SEVEN

"We have considered your request, Miss Beltane," Ben was saying as Uri and I walked towards him.

"Let's review the deal," I said.

"You only asked for one thing," Ben said.

"That's right. The truth," I said. "Where is Saint Peter buried?"

"I am prepared to tell you that..." Ben said, starting to pace the floor.

"Really?" I mouthed to Uri

"...on several conditions," Ben added.

"I told you what we were willing to do in return," I said. "Those were part of the deal."

"She give you her word, Ben," Uri said. "We leave Rome immediately and take the secret to our graves."

Ben scoffed. "You thought that would be enough?"

"I also said we wouldn't press charges against you and Antonio for the kidnapping and torture," I added.

"As long as we agreed to tell you the secret," Ben added.

"Yes," I said, getting frustrated that the conversation was going nowhere. "That was also part of it. You tell us the secret. In exchange, we leave Rome immediately, never press charges, never speak of it, take the secret to our graves. That was the whole deal. So what's the problem?"

Ben stopped pacing and eyed me. "Don't forget about the threat you made."

Uri looked at me. "Threat?"

"Oh yeah," I said, sheepishly. "I might have threatened the Pope."

"Might have?" Ben said.

Uri looked equally horrified and proud. "Mara, what did you say?"

Ben spoke for me. "Mara here told the Custodian that if we didn't tell her the secret of Saint Peter, she wouldn't stop until she discovered the truth for herself, and then she would unleash it on the world."

"On account of, and retribution for, our treatment while in your custody," I added.

Uri was grinning ear to ear, then allowed it to dissolve when he saw Ben scowling at him.

"The Holy See doesn't take too kindly to threats. And neither do I," Ben said.

"And I don't take too kindly to being kidnapped, interrogated, and tortured," I said.

"And for no reason," Uri said. "We did nothing wrong. You said so yourself. What you did to us was cruel and uncalled for."

"Not to mention unlawful," I said. "Officers of the law carried out illegal acts on two innocent, unsuspecting tourists. The Pope himself authorized it and played a part in it. And it all happened on your watch..."

I left the gravity of that statement sink in as silence filled the air.

"We could bury you, Ben," I said. "And the entire Vatican."

"Take the deal, Ben," Uri said.

Ben looked at each of us, contemplating. I couldn't tell if he was angry, impressed, or scared. Perhaps all three. Finally, he said, "You must both sign confidentiality agreements. That is a non-negotiable condition of the deal."

"Done," I said.

"The agreement says both of you must walk away and never speak to anyone about your time in Rome. You weren't even here, do you understand?"

"Fine," Uri and I said in unison.

"Second condition of the signed agreement: you permanently waive your right to legal action against any party involved in perpetuity."

"We already agreed to that," I said.

"Verbally," Ben clarified. "This will be in writing in a legally binding contract."

"Sure, whatever," I said.

"Third condition of the signed agreement: both of you are banned from ever returning to Italy, which of course includes Rome and Vatican City."

"As in forever?" Uri asked.

"In perpetuity," Ben said.

"That's not fair!" I objected.

"It's a condition you must agree to," Ben said. "And if you defy that condition and return, we will know."

"That's a little harsh," I said. "The whole country?"

"What I have to tell you is a truth more shocking than you could possibly imagine. We can't risk you being here. We are being more than generous by only asking for four things."

"There's another condition?" I asked, and Ben nodded. I looked at Uri, his solemn face telling me that if I wanted to know the truth I had to acquiesce.

"Fine," I said. "What is it?"

• • • •

"THE FOURTH AND FINAL condition of the signed agreement: you will not write your book, or any book, for that matter, pertaining to the secret I am prepared to reveal."

"Seriously?" I said.

Ben shrugged as if he didn't make the rules, he was just there to enforce them.

"Is there any room for negotiation?" Uri asked.

"I'm afraid not," Ben said. And that was all he said.

Uri and I looked at each other. He had a glint in his eye that told me his mind had already been made up. "Yes," his eyes were silently saying to me, "I am willing to make those sacrifices."

I, on the other hand, wasn't so sure. I felt my future career depended on writing this book. More than that, I was contractually obligated to hand in a manuscript. It didn't have to be this manuscript, but still—I'd worked so hard on this book, and now I'd have to start over. That was a very bitter pill to swallow.

And just as bad: never returning to Italy, ever?

These things, of course, were of no concern to Ben. After all, he was willing to divulge nothing less than a 2000-year-old secret that had the potential to start World War III.

Why? To what end? And what if it was a trap? What if I agreed to these things—these four life-altering things—and then the story Ben told us wound up being bogus, a way to get us out of the way, sweep the event under the rug so everyone could move on with their lives?

But if there was no secret to tell then why the disturbing phone calls to Uri, the clandestine meetings, the threats, the kidnapping...

I had no problem keeping mum on my time in Rome. I would begrudgingly agree to never return to Italy. And I had no intention of ever suing anyone, ever. But the book...

Uri eyed me, nodding his head at me as if to say, "Say yes!"

"I don't know, Uri..." I said. "This book meant everything to me."

"There will be other books, other opportunities...." he said. "Trust me."

"How can you know that?"

Uri looked at Ben. "May we have a moment, please?"

"As you wish," Ben said, backing away slowly.

Uri guided me a few paces out of Ben's earshot.

"What's going on, Uri?"

"There's something I need to tell you..." he began.

"Uh, OK. Right now?"

"Do you remember back in Jerusalem during our meeting with Lev when I said I had news that was unrelated to our mission in Rome?"

I had nearly forgotten but as the words came out of Uri's mouth, I remembered.

"Lev almost let the cat out of the bag," I said. "You refused to tell me. Something about it not being the right time or place."

"We had business to take care of first," Uri said. "And now that business has been taken care of."

I pointed at Ben, who'd begun pacing back and forth. "Not quite."

"True," Uri said, chuckling. "But now is the time."

"Why now?" I asked. "Ben is expecting an answer...I don't want to delay this any longer."

"Perhaps what I have to tell you will change your mind about Ben's offer..."

And with that, Uri launched into his news.

Uri had been offered a job, a once-in-a-lifetime opportunity by a major museum that was going to be opening a permanent exhibit featuring never-seen-before biblical-era artifacts. Display items would include portions of the Dead Sea Scrolls, stones from the Western Wall, and, coincidentally, ossuaries from the Talpiot tomb...

The museum was looking for a curator for this collection, an expert on ancient Israel and biblical times. They wanted Uri, and were willing to look past his transgressions with Jerusalem authorities concerning his Talpiot tomb incidents because, well, that meant he knew the Talpiot tomb better than anyone. He was perfect for the job.

And the job was in Philadelphia.

At the mention of this part, I swayed on my feet a bit, overwhelmed.

"Philadelphia?" I repeated, as if to make sure I wasn't in a waking dream.

Uri must have sensed my uneasiness because he said, "What it is? What's wrong?"

"It's perfect, Uri, really..."

"But...?"

"But what does this mean for you? Your life? Your career?"

"I've been a professor for nearly twenty years. I need a change. And I could go back to teaching anytime."

"Your whole life is in Jerusalem.." I said softly.

"My life is with you," he said, and kissed me on the cheek.

A tingle arose in my stomach, a twinge of anticipation mixed with a pang of uncertainty.

"Are you sure this is what you want, Uri?"

"Yes."

I paused, perhaps too long, because Uri said, "Don't think too much about it. Just say yes. To me, to this chance we've been given, to Ben's offer..."

Ben's offer.

It had temporarily been pushed to the back of my mind. I looked over at him, pacing back and forth, deep in thought.

I sighed deeply, choked down the realization that I'd never write the book I came to Rome to write, swallowed any lingering doubts, then gave Uri my answer.

The answer was yes.

"Let's do it," I said. "Let's do all of it."

Uri and I locked eyes and as we did, Uri said, "We're ready, Ben."

Ben approached and stood in front of us.

"We want the truth," I said.

"Are you sure?" he asked.

I looked at Uri and he nodded. "Absolutely."

Ben walked over to the door and banged on it three times. A young man entered, carrying a big cloth satchel. He handed it to Ben, who carried it over to the table and pulled the contents out. Inside were two bound documents, identical in size and thickness, each bearing the papal seal. Uri and I gathered around Ben. He slid one of the documents across the table to me and the other to Uri, and then handed us each a pen. As he did this, he spoke.

"You understand that everything I'm about to tell you is confidential, that you swear an oath to the Vatican and the Holy See that you will not share any of this knowledge with anyone, at any time, ever."

Uri and I nodded.

"...and that you agree to the terms set forth to you moments ago, as they are stated in the documents you are about to sign..."

"Yes," Uri and I said in unison.

"...and that by breaking this oath you would be jeopardizing your lives, as well as those of the Pope, the members of the Holy See, and those of the Ordo Fratrum Minorum...."

"What?" I said incredulously.

Ben eyed me as if we were past the point of questioning or negotiation.

"Okay, fine," I said, and Ben looked over at Uri for his confirmation.

"Agreed," Uri said.

"And lastly," Ben said, "that neither myself, nor the Pope, nor any members of the Holy See or the Ordo Fratrum Minorum can be held responsible for anything that might happen to you should you break your oath."

"Seriously?" I said.

Ben furrowed his brows at me as he were about to scold a misbehaving child. "Do not underestimate the power of the information I am about to give you."

I heeded the weight of his words, the look on his face, the underlying fear I heard in his voice.

"Mara, do you swear?" Ben asked.

Uri's brown eyes burned into me, begging me to concede.

"I swear," I said.

"Uri?" Ben asked.

Uri kept his eyes on me. "I swear."

And with that, Ben revealed the truth—the unbelievable secret—of Saint Peter.

EPILOGUE

O*ne year later*
    The bookstore was surprisingly busy for a rainy Friday afternoon. I stood behind a table near the front of the store, arranging books in a neat pile. I picked up one of the books, just recently published the week before, and stared at the title.

It wasn't the book I had expected to write.

I'd intended to write a thriller about the life and death of Saint Peter. But fate had other plans for my career—and for my personal life.

I was home in Philadelphia, at a book signing, the first stop on a two-week tour that would take me across the country, promoting the new book. I had long since sold my condo and bought a home with Dr. Uri Nevon. He'd started his new job and I had started a new book and we were starting a new life together.

A bookstore employee approached me and we made small talk for a few minutes until a young woman approached the table.

"I'm a big fan," she said, picking up one of the books. "I've read all your books."

"Thank you," I said. "I hope you enjoy this newest one. Would you like me to sign it for you?"

She finished reading the description on the back of the book, furrowed her brow, then looked up at me in confusion.

"I read on your blog that your next book was supposed to be about Saint Peter," she said.

"Turns out there was nothing to tell," I said. Then I leaned over and whispered as if sharing a secret, "This book is way better than that book would've been."

The woman looked confused by my answer but then her face lit up and she handed the book to me to sign. We chatted for a few minutes and as she walked away a familiar figure came into view.

"Better than Saint Peter?" he said, approaching from my right near the magazine racks. "I'll be the judge of that."

Dr. Giovanni Maderno.

We greeted and hugged. Then I rummaged through my bag for the book I had set aside just for him. I had signed it, "Thanks for being an inspiring tour guide and an amazing friend."

Giovanni read the inscription, smiled and bowed. "You're most welcome, Mrs. Nevon."

I cringed at the comment but understood his intention. "The ceremony tomorrow will not involve any name changes," I gently reminded him. "But it does involve my sincere gratitude for your travels from Italy."

"I'm teasing, as you know," Giovanni said.

I smiled. "Uri and I are so pleased and honored you'll be there to witness our nuptials."

He looked at me all-knowingly. "I told you it was *amore*."

"Yes, you did."

Giovanni looked at the book again. "Well, it's not Saint Peter, but I'd say you chose one hell of an alternative. I can't wait to read it."

"Thank you."

"So tell me, what adventure did this book take you on?"

"Read it and find out."